DISNEY

PIRATES *of the* CARIBBEAN
AT WORLD'S END

Adapted by T.T. Sutherland and Elizabeth Rudnick

Based on the screenplay written by
Ted Elliott & Terry Rossio
Based on characters created by Ted Elliott & Terry Rossio
and Stuart Beattie and Jay Wolpert
Based on Walt Disney's Pirates of the Caribbean
Produced by Jerry Bruckheimer
Directed by Gore Verbinski

DISNEP PRESS
New York

For information address Disney Press, 114 Fifth Avenue,
New York, New York 10011-5690.
Printed in the United States of America
First Edition
1 3 5 7 9 10 8 6 4 2
This book is set in 13-point Charlotte Book.
Library of Congress Catalog Card Number: 2007902440
ISBN-13: 978-1-4231-1208-2
ISBN-10: 1-4231-1208-3
Visit DISNEYPIRATES.COM

Chapter 1

"There be something on the seas that even the most staunch and bloodthirsty pirates have come to fear. . . ."

From his spot high in the crow's nest, a pirate trained his spyglass on the horizon.

Nothing. No sign of any ship besides his own and the two they traveled with. The Caribbean Sea was calm, the bright sun sparkling off the ocean waves. Everything was peaceful.

So why did he have such a strong sense of foreboding?

He lifted his spyglass again. This time he could see a smudge on the horizon. It might be a ship sailing toward them. Worse, it might be an East India Trading Company ship.

The pirate knew what would happen if they

were taken by Company agents. He had heard stories of the recent executions . . . pirates hanged by the dozen, the *thunk* of the gallows' trapdoor the last sound they ever heard. And in the last few months, the executions were becoming more and more frequent. The East India Trading Company was intent on wiping out the Pirates of the Caribbean—and beyond.

The pirate leaned over to call down to the captain. If it was an East India Trading Company ship, they would have to make a run for it. But, as he looked down, he saw a shape in the water beside them. A dark shape, rising up—and rising fast.

"CAPTAIN!" he shouted.

It was too late.

With an explosion of ocean spray, the shape burst through the surface of the water. First, pale masts rose into the air. Then came the rails and wooden hull, crusted with coral and shells. A carved skeletal, winged female rode on the bow.

It was something out of the darkest of nightmares. It was something pirates spoke of in hushed and frightened tones.

It was the *Flying Dutchman*.

The ship opened her cannon ports as she surfaced. With a loud explosion, cannonballs blazed into the side of the pirate ship. The pirates on all three ships ran to their stations, trying to load and return fire, but the *Flying Dutchman* was too fast, too close, too powerful.

The attack was over in minutes.

Smoke curled over the burning wreckage. Bodies of dead pirates drifted past loose barrels and blackened wood.

The *Flying Dutchman* sailed through, regal, untouched. Unstoppable.

On the distant horizon, another ship appeared. It was an East India Trading Company ship, the *Endeavour*, carrying Lord Cutler Beckett, Admiral James Norrington, and Governor Weatherby Swann.

In the captain's cabin of the *Dutchman*, Davy Jones sat at his pipe organ. His scaly skin glistened in the dim light while the octopus tentacles that hung from his face moved back and forth gently over the keys, filling the room with a melancholy sound. With a sigh, he lifted one of the tentacle fingers on his right hand to his eye and discovered a tear forming. Sadness and emotion . . . That could only mean one thing. He glanced up with a scowl.

Above the cabin, Admiral Norrington and Lord Beckett were coming aboard with a contingent of marines. The marines seemed afraid to be standing on the deck of the *Flying Dutchman*. And their fears were well founded. The crew of the *Dutchman* was covered in barnacles and scales— more monster than human.

"Steady, men," said Norrington, noting his crew's unease. "We stand aboard a seagoing vessel, no more and no less. You will compose yourselves as marines."

As he spoke, several of the men heaved a chest over the rail and onto the deck of the *Dutchman*. This was what they were here to guard: the Dead Man's Chest. Inside was the still-beating heart of Davy Jones.

From his spot on the deck, Lord Beckett smiled. He had waited and plotted for a great length of time to be standing where he was now, with Jones at his command.

Beckett knew that Davy Jones captained the fastest ship on the ocean. The crew of the

Dutchman were all bound to Davy Jones for a hundred years, body and soul. Davy Jones himself was immortal. After his true love had broken his heart, he had cut out the offending organ and put it in the Dead Man's Chest, which he buried at *Isla Cruces*. Nobody could harm him unless they had his heart.

Which was precisely why Lord Beckett had spent so much energy searching for it.

To begin with, he'd arrested a blacksmith named Will Turner and the governor of Port Royal's daughter, Elizabeth Swann, on their wedding day. In exchange for their freedom, he'd sent Will to get a compass belonging to the pesky pirate, Captain Jack Sparrow. This particular Compass pointed not north, but to whatever your heart desired most. Once Beckett had the Compass, he thought it would lead him straight to the Dead Man's Chest.

Things hadn't worked out quite as Beckett planned, but they still had worked out very much in his favor. Will, Elizabeth, and Jack had found the way to *Isla Cruces* before Beckett. But Norrington, who had joined Sparrow's crew after losing his navy position for letting the pirate escape hanging, was able to slip in and steal Davy Jones's heart. He brought it back to Port Royal and relinquished it to Beckett. Immediately, Norrington was reinstated in the Royal Navy and promoted to admiral.

So while Beckett hadn't gotten the Compass, he now had something of far greater value and with infinitely more power: the heart of Davy Jones . . . and complete control over the *Flying Dutchman*. With the power of this ship, Beckett— and the East India Trading Company—could rule the seas. Better yet, the *Black Pearl*—the only ship that could ever be a match for the *Dutchman*— had been pulled under by Jones's own pet monster, the Kraken.

"Go, the lot of you—and take that with you!" Jones bellowed, appearing from belowdecks. Shaking with anger, he strode up to Norrington but stayed a safe distance away from the chest. The closer the heart was to him, the more emotion he felt. Jones wouldn't feel safe until the heart was far away from him.

"I will not have that infernal thing on my ship!" Davy Jones shouted.

"Oh, I'm sorry to hear that," Lord Beckett said coldly. "Because I will. Because it seems to be the only way to ensure that this ship does as directed by the Company."

Jones gripped the rail of the ship with the claw that formed his left hand. The long tentacles of his beard writhed with fury.

Beckett nodded at Norrington, who led the marines below with the chest.

"The *Dutchman* sails as its captain commands," Jones growled.

"And the captain is to sail it as commanded," Beckett responded. "This is no longer your world, Jones. The immaterial has become . . . immaterial. I would have thought you'd learned that when I ordered you to kill your pet."

Jones winced, remembering the Kraken. The powerful sea monster that had killed Jack Sparrow and dragged the *Pearl* under was now dead, one of the first casualties of Beckett's ruthless campaign against the "uncivilized" seas.

At that moment, Governor Swann stepped forward. From aboard the *Endeavour*, he had watched the destruction of the pirate ships with horror. Not a soul had been left alive. The ships had been blasted to smithereens. His blood boiling, the governor had followed Beckett and Norrington onto the *Dutchman*.

"Did you give these ships opportunity to surrender?" the governor, his face pale beneath his white wig, demanded of Davy Jones.

Jones smirked. "We let them see us. Methinks that opportunity enough."

Swann was outraged. "My daughter could have been aboard one of them!" he cried. "That alone is cause to exercise restraint!" The governor had been searching for Elizabeth for months, ever since he helped her escape her cell in Port Royal and saw her flee into the dark night. He knew she would have gone to find Will and Jack among the pirates. But since that night, he had neither seen nor heard from her. By traveling with Beckett and Norrington, he had hoped to find her . . . before she was caught and executed as a pirate.

But Beckett had different reasons to be displeased with Jones's disobedience.

"We need prisoners to interrogate," Beckett snapped at Jones. "Which works best when they are *alive*."

"I am exterminating pirates," Jones said, "as commanded by the Company." He gave a mocking bow, then turned to Swann. "And your daughter is dead. Pulled under with the *Black Pearl*—by my pet. Did Lord Beckett not tell you that?" Jones grinned mirthlessly.

Swann stood for a moment in shock. Lord Beckett had been lying to him all this time. Elizabeth was dead. He whirled and ran for the cabin.

Lord Beckett gave Jones a dark look and followed him.

Norrington was just placing the key in the lock of the chest when Swann suddenly grabbed him and pulled him around.

"Did you know?" Swann yelled, shaking Norrington by his lapels. "Did you know?"

"Governor Swann!" barked Lord Beckett from the doorway. Swann shoved Norrington away. He seized a bayonet from the closest marine and brandished it. Norrington grabbed his arms, restraining him.

Beckett spoke sharply to the marines. "Out. Everyone."

The soldiers glanced at Norrington, who nodded. They filed out, leaving the chest alone with Swann, Beckett, Norrington, Jones, and Beckett's aide, Mercer.

"Governor Swann," Beckett said soothingly, "believe me . . . I only sought to spare you from the pain—"

"You only sought to use my political connections to further your own cause!" Swann spat. "The worst pirate who ever sailed has more honor than you. Even Jack Sparrow had honor."

Beckett smiled thinly. "Jack Sparrow is no more. And was never more than selfish desire cloaked in romantic fictions. A legend we're well rid of."

Norrington was still confused. Why was Governor Swann so upset? "You knew Sparrow was dead," he said to Swann.

"Not him," Swann said. "Elizabeth!"

Admiral Norrington gasped. He felt numb with shock. While it was true Elizabeth had made her choice long ago—turning her back on their betrothal—Norrington still cared deeply for the headstrong woman. The news of her death struck him to the core. His grip loosened on the governor, and Swann was able to pull himself free and throw open the chest, revealing the beating heart of Davy Jones.

"No!" Jones shouted.

Swann raised his bayonet high.

But before he could strike, Jones's voice cut through his agony. "Are you prepared to take up my burden, then?" the immortal captain hissed. "If you slay the heart, then yours must take its place—and you must take mine. The *Dutchman* must always have a captain."

Governor Swann hesitated. He had not known about the dreadful consequences of stabbing Jones's heart. No one would willingly choose that kind of eternal captivity. But if it would stop Lord Beckett . . . Swann glanced at the aristocrat. Beckett spread his hands in a gesture that indicated the choice was Swann's. Swann turned back to the chest, but Norrington caught his arm and yanked the bayonet away from him.

"Let me!" Swann implored.

Norrington shook his head. "Elizabeth would not have wanted this," he said firmly.

The governor's shoulders slumped. Norrington was right. His anger drained away, replaced by deep grief. He had failed his own flesh and blood.

"Elizabeth . . ." he said sadly.

Norrington placed an arm over his shoulders and gently steered the governor out the door. Beckett, Jones, and Mercer watched them leave.

"You're dismissed, Captain," Beckett said.

Jones reluctantly followed the others out. Beckett and Mercer looked at each other for a long moment. Beckett crossed to the chest and closed it softly, turning the key with a contemplative look.

"They know," said Mercer.

"I can order Admiral Norrington's silence," Beckett said. "He'll obey; it's what he does."

"And the governor?" Mercer asked.

"Yes, well," Lord Beckett mused. "Every man should have a secret he carries to his grave."

And as he smiled knowingly, the *Dutchman* sailed on, across the bright blue Caribbean Sea, ready to bring more dark death and bloody destruction to the next pirate ship it found.

As long as Lord Beckett and the East India Trading Company controlled the heart of Davy Jones, no pirate was safe. It was only a matter of time before every pirate in the Caribbean was exterminated.

Chapter 2

Lord Cutler Beckett was wrong about one thing.

Elizabeth Swann was still very much alive.

She had seen the *Black Pearl* dragged to the depths of Davy Jones's Locker with Jack Sparrow aboard. And she knew that no matter what stories were told, it was *her* fault he was dead. After fleeing *Isla Cruces*, the *Pearl* had come under attack by the Kraken. Why? Because Jack had been marked by the Black Spot. Its presence on his hand meant there was nowhere on the sea he could hide. And so the Kraken had found him.

At first, Jack fled, taking a longboat and heading to shore alone. But then he had a change of heart. He had returned to his ship to help Will, Elizabeth, and his crew. However, Elizabeth knew that if Jack were with them, the Kraken would not stop hunting them—and they would all die. So she distracted Jack with a kiss and then chained him to the mast of the *Black Pearl*, leaving him there to die.

In the aftermath, Elizabeth had been racked by guilt. She was determined to fix things. Along with Will and Jack's crew, she had gone to see a powerful mystic named Tia Dalma, who had helped Jack in the past.

Tia Dalma lived far up the Pantano River in a bayou that smelled of mystery and magic. The air was never quite clear, and, as they had made their way slowly toward Tia Dalma's shack, it had been hard not to feel watched.

In the dim twilight, Elizabeth, Will, and the remaining members of Jack's crew had rowed their way slowly up to Tia Dalma's rickety front porch. With a great deal of effort and an even greater amount of fear, they had made their way inside, where Tia Dalma waited.

There, the mystic had told them there was indeed a way to bring Jack Sparrow back to the world of the living. But they would need the help of an old enemy . . . Captain Barbossa, the man who had stolen the *Pearl* from Sparrow many years before. Before their run-in with Jones, Will and Elizabeth had helped Jack reclaim the *Pearl*, and

Jack had killed Barbossa on *Isla de Muerta*. But now Tia Dalma had brought Barbossa back from the dead for reasons of her own. And she knew he could help them bring back Jack as well.

Singapore's harbor was a dark and shadowy place, full of secrets, unkempt pirates, and flashing knives. Tall ships and smaller junks crowded together around ramshackle docks. Wooden boards creaked in the wind, and hanging lamps cast flickering shadows over the people who darted through narrow, winding streets.

A small boat drifted along the gloomy byways. In the bow, a cloaked figure used a long pole to maneuver the boat through a maze of pylons below the docks. The figure's voice drifted eerily in the darkness, singing an old pirate song.

"The bell has been raised from its watery grave . . . do you hear its sepulchral tone?" she sang. *"A call to all, pay heed the squall and turn your sails toward home!"*

The boat passed below a lantern, revealing the figure's face. It was Elizabeth Swann. Although she appeared calm, her large brown eyes darted back and forth, taking in the city. It had nothing like the manicured streets and stately mansions of her youth or her time in Port Royal. The corseted dresses she had once worn had no place here—the brown, shapeless cloak she had on was far more appropriate.

As her longboat floated under the docks, Elizabeth passed an old woman crouched over a mess of fish remains. Nearby, a man was blowing glass at a coal fire, the glowing orange-red light reflecting off the round glass shape. An explosion to her right made her jump; she saw a dazzling pinwheel spin out of a fireworks shed, sparks flying. A boy chased it, stamping down the sparks.

With a shiver, Elizabeth saw the shadow of a monkey race by. She moved forward, still singing, until she reached a dock where she tied up the boat and climbed out.

"Yo ho, haul together," she sang as she tied up the line. Suddenly she stopped and ducked her head. A troop of East India Trading Company agents was passing by, led by Beckett's aide, Mercer. They were exactly who she *didn't* want to hear her song. She wanted the song to identify her as a pirate—but only to *fellow* pirates.

A few moments later, the march of their

boots faded away. Elizabeth resumed her song.

"Raise the colors high! Heave ho . . ."

". . . thieves and beggars," a new voice joined in. *"Never say we die."*

Elizabeth rose to her feet as a man stepped out of the darkness of a large sewer pipe. Two armed guards flanked him. He was tall and imposing, his sinewy muscles rippling under his dark robes. He had a menacing look in his eyes and a wicked sword at his side.

Despite the man's formidable presence, Elizabeth sighed in relief. This was Tai Huang, the man she was looking for. Or at least, the man who could take her to the man she was looking for. Tai Huang was second in command to Sao Feng, the fearsome Pirate Lord of Singapore.

Tai Huang narrowed his eyes, looking her up and down.

"A dangerous song to be singing," he said ominously, "for any who are ignorant of its meaning." He stepped closer. "Particularly a woman. Particularly a woman alone."

"What makes you think she's alone?"

Tai Huang and his guards turned at the sound of the new voice. Barbossa was standing

17

behind them, a smile on his weather-beaten face.

"You protect her?" Tai Huang asked.

"What makes you think I need protection?" Elizabeth replied with a hiss. Tai Huang froze. Elizabeth's knife was pressed to his throat.

Barbossa tsk-tsked.

"Your master is expecting us," he said to Tai Huang. He added, pointedly, to Elizabeth: "And an unexpected death would cast a slight pall on our meeting." He eyed her knife. Slowly she lowered it but did not sheath it.

Tai Huang rubbed his neck and studied the old pirate. "You're Captain Barbossa," he said.

"Aye," Barbossa agreed. "And she be Elizabeth Swann. And Sao Feng has promised us safe passage."

Huang nodded thoughtfully. "For as long as it suits him," he said in a dark voice. He turned in a whirl of robes to lead them away, then abruptly held up his hand. Everyone stopped short.

The sound of boots heralded the passage of more East India Trading Company men. Tai Huang waited until the agents turned a corner, and then he signaled the others to follow him into the mouth of the large sewer pipe.

As Elizabeth and Barbossa vanished into the darkness, something peculiar was happening not too far away.

On one of the many dilapidated bridges that crossed over the canals and waterways of Singapore, a pair of East India Trading Company agents was standing guard. Had they looked over the edge into the water, they might have seen a line of coconuts floating by.

But below the coconuts was something that would have interested the agents very much indeed. Underneath each coconut was a member of the nefarious Captain Jack Sparrow's crew.

As the coconuts floated into the darkness under the bridge, one rose out of the water, revealing the top of the pirate Ragetti's head. He was wearing the coconut shell as a helmet, hiding him from sight up above. His one good eye darted back and forth, while his wooden one stared blankly ahead. Following behind him were Pintel, Gibbs, Cotton, and Marty.

When they were safely hidden in the

shadows below the bridge, they took off their coconut helmets and swam over to a metal grate. From the oilskin bundles they carried, they produced large rasps which could be used to file through the bars of the grate.

Then they waited.

Squeak, squeeeeak. The East India Trading Company agents snapped to attention and peered into the gloom. What was that sound?

A moment later, a woman trundled out of the darkness pushing a cart with squeaky wheels. The cart carried several birdcages holding twittering canaries, clanking bottles filled with mystery potions, and bags of flour. On top of the cages was a colorful parrot, and riding alongside the bird was a monkey turning the crank of an organ.

This was what Jack's crew had been waiting for. The organ's music, the squeaking wheels, and the clattering sounds of the cart were all loud enough to hide any noise from below. It was time to act. The pirates set to work on filing through the bars of the grate.

The cart rolled closer and closer. The agents exchanged a suspicious glance. They stepped forward to stop the cart.

The music stopped. Down below, the pirates froze.

One of the agents pulled out his sword.

"You can't be here," the agent said gruffly to the woman.

She lifted her face. Although they did not know it, the woman was Tia Dalma. She leaned toward the agent who had spoken to her and whispered in an eerie voice, "Your mother always knew it be you who threw the linens down the well."

The agent jumped back, spooked. He stared at the old woman in fear.

"How did you know that?" he demanded.

She grinned, revealing a mouthful of blackened teeth. "The canaries," she hissed.

Both agents backed away. They didn't know what witchcraft was at work here, but they wanted nothing to do with it. "Jack" the Monkey picked up the organ again and went back to grinding, the music whirling brightly as the pirates resumed their sawing down below.

Not too far away, Tai Huang was leading Barbossa and Elizabeth through a decrepit bathhouse. The bathhouse served as Sao Feng's hideout and was well protected. Elizabeth glanced about her, all her senses on high alert. Anyone they passed could be a pirate . . . or worse, an employee of the East India Trading Company.

She tugged on Barbossa's sleeve. "Have we heard anything from Will?" she whispered.

Barbossa shook his head. "The whelp is more than capable of taking care of himself," he pointed out. "But you—in the presence of Sao Feng you'll be wanting to show a bit more diffidence than is your custom." He winked.

"He's that terrifying, is he?" Elizabeth asked.

"He's much like myself," Barbossa answered, "absent my merciful nature and sense of fair play." He grinned, and Elizabeth shivered.

Tai Huang stepped in front of a door, rapping a series of sharp knocks in a coded signal. A slit in the door slid open and a pair of eyes appeared. The eyes studied them. After a minute, the slit closed and, with the sound of bolts moving and hinges creaking, the door opened.

As Elizabeth and Barbossa stepped inside a small entry room, Tai Huang swung around, blocking their path.

"No weapons," he said. "Remove them, please." Elizabeth could tell from his tone that the "please" did not make his sentence any more of a request. It was an order.

"Of course," Barbossa said cheerfully. He handed over his pistol and his sword, and Elizabeth followed suit. But as they stepped forward, Tai Huang held up his hand and eyed Elizabeth.

"Did you think because she is a woman, we would not suspect her of treachery?" he asked. "Remove, please."

Elizabeth sighed and pulled off her coat, revealing two more hidden swords in scabbards tucked into the lining.

She started forward again—but Tai Huang stopped her. "Remove. Please," he repeated.

Elizabeth tried to protest, but it was no use. She was forced to turn over each of her hidden weapons, one by one. To add insult to injury, she was also ordered to change into a robe that would allow no weapons to remain hidden. Glaring at the men around her, Elizabeth cinched the belt on her blue silk robe tighter and tugged it down, hoping to cover her legs a bit more.

Finally, scowling and completely unarmed, she followed Barbossa and Tai Huang deeper into the bathhouse.

As they walked the maze of leaky, rusted pipes past algae-crusted tubs and half-naked pirates, Elizabeth studied her surroundings. The pirates here all worked for Sao Feng. And they each bore his symbol: a dragon tattoo.

At last they reached a room that was cleaner and warmer than the rest. The Pirate Lord of Singapore was just stepping out of his tub. Silently, two attractive female attendants dressed him in all the glory of his pirate regalia.

Elizabeth stared at the man's scarred and weathered face, looking for a sign of weakness. But the powerful Lord's eyes were dark and cold, revealing nothing. From the corners of his eyes ran a pair of old scars that heightened his dangerous demeanor.

A long moment passed. Sao Feng did not seem to have noticed their presence . . . or else he was deliberately ignoring them. Finally, Barbossa realized it was up to him to speak first.

"Captain Sao Feng," he said smoothly, "thank you for granting me this audience."

Sao Feng looked up as if he'd just spotted them. "Captain Barbossa!" he said. "Welcome to Singapore." With a gesture, he turned to the nearest guard and said, "More steam."

The guard banged on the wall twice, and a burst of steam billowed out of the pipes.

"I understand that you have a request to make of me . . . ?" he said to Barbossa.

"And a proposal to make to you," Barbossa replied. "I've a venture underway, and I find myself in need of a ship and a crew."

Sao Feng looked at Barbossa with a sly smile. "And you consider me worthy of such an honor? A ship and a crew . . ." He chuckled. "That's an odd coincidence."

"Because you happen to have a ship and a crew you don't need?" Elizabeth said saucily. Barbossa gave her a warning glance, but Sao Feng only smiled wider, the scars at the corners of his eyes almost disappearing.

"No," he said. "Because earlier this day, not far from here, a thief broke into my most revered uncle's temple, and tried to make off with these."

Sao Feng strode across the room to a wizened old man in long robes who was clutching a set of ancient charts to his chest. The Pirate Lord reached for the charts but had to tug on them several times with a stern expression before the old man would relinquish them.

"Navigational charts," Sao Feng continued, turning back to Barbossa and Elizabeth and holding the charts aloft with a flourish. "The route to the Farthest Gate," he said softly, watching their faces for a reaction. "Wouldn't it be amazing if this venture of yours took you to the world beyond this one?"

Barbossa swallowed. "It would strain credulity, at that," he blustered.

Sao Feng gazed at him levelly. Then with a nod, he signaled to two guards near one of the baths. The guards leaned over and hauled a figure out from under the water.

The prisoner was none other than Will Turner.

Chapter 3

Will Turner was very unhappy.

There was something Elizabeth did not know.

Will had seen her kissing Jack on the *Pearl*.

Of course, he didn't know that she had done it to trick Jack. He didn't know that she had chained Jack to the mast. He thought Jack had *chosen* to go down with his own ship. He also thought that Elizabeth must no longer love him. Will was convinced she was now in love with Jack.

So Will did not particularly care that Jack Sparrow was dead. In fact, he probably would have left him that way, if it were up to him. But Will had his own mission, and, unfortunately, it involved helping Jack.

After Beckett had ordered Will to hunt down Jack and his Compass, Will had wound up on the *Flying Dutchman*—thanks to Jack's scheming. Will had been Davy Jones's prisoner for a short while. In that time, he had discovered something terrible. His own father, the pirate known as "Bootstrap Bill" Turner, was enslaved aboard the *Dutchman*. Bootstrap Bill had once been a member of the *Black Pearl's* crew, but he had wound up in the depths of the ocean after refusing to take part in Barbossa's mutiny against Jack. Cursed by the Aztec Gold and doomed to be trapped there forever, he had been more than willing to bargain with Jones when the tentacled captain found him. But the price had been terrible: one hundred years of servitude.

Bootstrap Bill was like the rest of the *Dutchman* crew now—covered in barnacles and crustaceans, a slave to Davy Jones. As time went by, he was gradually losing himself and becoming a part of the ship—literally. Long before the hundred years were up, he'd be lost forever, just another tortured soul swallowed up by the ship.

After their reunion, Will had sworn to rescue his father. He had made Bill a solemn promise: he would return to the *Dutchman* and free him, no matter what it took.

But in order to do that, he needed the fastest ship on the seas, the only one that could catch the *Flying Dutchman*. Which meant he needed the *Black Pearl*. And that was why he was on this quest to save Jack. Wherever Jack was . . . the *Pearl* would be there, too.

Now, soaking wet and defenseless, Will found himself in the middle of Sao Feng's hideout. The Pirate Lord grabbed Will by the hair and dragged him to Barbossa and Elizabeth.

"This is the thief," he snarled. "Is his face familiar to you?"

Elizabeth managed not to react. She and Barbossa both steeled their faces to look impassive, as if they had never seen Will before in their lives.

Sao Feng studied them and then shrugged. "No?" He picked up a large metal spike on a nearby table. This was a fid, a sharp tool used for winding ropes together. Sao Feng brushed the sharp end of the fid along the edge of Will's face. "Then I guess he has no further need for it."

He moved the fid sharply toward Will, and

Elizabeth tensed. She couldn't stop herself. After all, the man Sao Feng was threatening was her true love and fiancé.

Sao Feng saw her reaction and frowned darkly. His suspicions were confirmed. Now he was sure they were working together. The two of them had come to beg from him, while their friend snuck around to stab him in the back.

"You come into my city," Sao Feng growled, "you seek my indulgence and largesse, and you betray my hospitality?" His voice rose. "You betray *me*?"

Barbossa bowed and spread his hands. "Sao Feng," he tried, "I assure you, I had no idea—"

"—that he would get caught," Sao Feng interrupted.

Barbossa winced. The Pirate Lord had a point.

Sao Feng narrowed his eyes, tapping the charts against his chest. He was putting the pieces of the puzzle together. "You intend to attempt a voyage to Davy Jones's Locker," he said. "And I cannot help but wonder: why?"

Barbossa sighed. It was time to be completely honest—not something that came naturally to pirates. The ex-captain of the *Pearl* drew a silver piece of eight out of his pocket and tossed it to Sao Feng, who caught it in midair and examined it.

A new, troubled look crossed the Pirate Lord's face. "A piece of eight," he murmured. He looked up at Barbossa. "It's true, then?"

"Aye," Barbossa answered. "The time is upon us. We must convene the Brethren Court."

Sao Feng banged on the wall. "More steam!" he bellowed.

Below the floorboards, the boiler and bellows system was normally worked by two attendants. But the attendants were now tied up. They had been overpowered by Jack's crew of pirates, who had crept in through the steam tunnels. At Sao Feng's cry, Cotton hurried over to the boiler mechanism and quickly figured out how it worked. Soon, steam was billowing up through the vents.

The other pirates once again unrolled their oilskin bundles, revealing swords, pistols, and grenades. They began placing the grenades in the floor joists, preparing to set off a massive explosion.

Gibbs, Jack Sparrow's first mate, and Ragetti

exchanged glances. They were underneath the room where their friends were confronting Sao Feng. If things didn't go the way they were supposed to . . . then this hidden group of pirates was the only chance Will, Elizabeth, and Barbossa had to make it out . . . alive.

Sao Feng breathed in the steam. "The Court has not met in my lifetime," he said.

"Nor mine," Barbossa said.

Sao Feng's hand reached up and caressed the rope pendant he wore around his neck. "And when last it did, my father told me, it ended . . . badly."

"But the time before that, it produced the Code," Barbossa pointed out, "which has served us well . . . and it was the very first meeting that gave us no less than rule of the sea herself, didn't it?" Barbossa was referring to the legend of Calypso, an ancient sea goddess. The nine Pirate Lords of the first Court had captured Calypso and bound her in human form. When she could no longer send storms to destroy them, their own rule over the sea had become absolute. It had been the turning point for pirates everywhere.

The imprisonment of Calypso meant that they could be the lords of the sea.

Barbossa's voice turned darker and more serious. "And now that rule is being challenged."

"The East India Trading Company," Sao Feng hissed. He, too, had seen the devastation wrought by the agents of the Company. He had heard of the mass executions, and he had lost some of his own men to their terrible slaughter. He knew that pirates were in grave danger of losing not only their lives but their reign over the seas . . . forever.

"Lord Cutler Beckett is a pox on us all," Barbossa said, nodding.

Sao Feng began pacing back and forth. "There is a price on all our heads, it is true," he said. "It seems the only way a pirate can turn a profit anymore . . . is by betraying other pirates." He gave Will a significant look, then turned back to Barbossa. "But pirates are either captain or crew, and nine squabbling captains trying to chart a course is eight captains too many."

He shook his head. "Against the Company, what value is the Brethren Court? What can any of us do?"

Elizabeth couldn't keep quiet any longer. "You can fight," she cried.

Everyone turned to stare at her. Her frustration was boiling over. What was wrong with these pirates? Couldn't they see what was happening out there? Didn't they believe in the Pirate Code? Didn't they want to take back the sea—*their* sea?

"You are Sao Feng, the Pirate Lord of Singapore," she said boldly, stepping forward. "You command in the Age of Piracy, where bold captains sail free waters, where waves are not measured in feet but increments of fear, and those who pass the test become legend." A large pirate with a dragon tattoo tried to pull her back, but she shook him off and stepped even closer to Sao Feng.

With passion in her voice, she added, "Would you have that era come to an end on your watch?"

Sao Feng regarded her with an impassive expression.

"But here you are," Elizabeth continued scornfully. "Your ships crowd the harbor, rotting on their lines, while you cower in your bathwater!"

The Pirate Lord's eyebrows twitched, and

Elizabeth fell silent. Had she gone too far? She held her breath as he circled her slowly, eyeing her like a predator might study an interesting bit of prey.

"Elizabeth Swann," he said, "there is more to you than meets the eye, isn't there? And the eye does not go wanting." He gave her a charming smile, and she was shocked when she found herself smiling back.

Sao Feng turned back to Barbossa. "But I can't help but notice you have failed to answer my question." If the talk of the Brethren Court and Elizabeth's call to arms had been intended to distract Sao Feng, it had failed. He pressed once again: "What is it you seek in Davy Jones's Locker?"

"Jack Sparrow," said a voice from across the room. Will Turner shook the wet hair out of his face and stood up straighter. His gaze was level and unafraid as he stared at the Lord.

Sao Feng froze. Silence fell. Barbossa looked pained.

"He's one of the Pirate Lords," Will said.

One of Sao Feng's attendants, a girl named Park, giggled, but hid her smile when Sao Feng glared at her. The other, Lian, seemed to be hiding a pleased expression as well. Both of them had clearly encountered the legendary Jack Sparrow before.

Will and Elizabeth could both see how angry Sao Feng was to hear the name Jack Sparrow. A vein throbbed in his temple as he fought to keep his voice calm.

"The only reason I would want Jack Sparrow returned from the realm of the dead," the Pirate Lord hissed, "is so I can send him back myself."

Barbossa rolled his eyes and glared at Will. "Exactly why we preferred his name go unmentioned," he said pointedly.

"So you admit you have deceived me," Sao Feng said. His eyes scanned the room, and suddenly he spotted something suspicious. In the billowing waves of steam and heat, the dragon tattoo on one of his men was melting. It was a fake! There was another spy here—one who had gone so far as to infiltrate his organization. The man went by the name Steng, and he had joined Sao Feng's pirates some time earlier. Through narrowed eyes, Sao Feng now glared at the man. Was he part of Barbossa's group as well? The layers of deception appeared to be growing deeper.

Barbossa hadn't noticed Sao Feng's scrutiny of Steng. "Jack Sparrow holds one of the nine Pieces of Eight!" he said. "He failed to pass it along to a successor before he died."

As Barbossa spoke, Sao Feng caught the eye of Tai Huang. With a subtle gesture, he indicated Steng. Barbossa kept speaking: "And so we must go and fetch him back—"

"WEAPONS!" Sao Feng bellowed suddenly.

All at once, the Singapore pirates sprang into action. Before Will, Elizabeth, or Barbossa could move, the dragon-tattooed guards around them had seized swords and pistols from under the water in the tubs. Within moments, the three were surrounded by a ring of weaponry, all pointed at them.

Barbossa held up his empty hands. "I assure you, our intentions are strictly honorable—" he began. But he was interrupted by the sound of swords sliding up through the floorboards. The pirates below had realized that things were going wrong and had acted quickly to arm their crew up above. Within seconds, Elizabeth had seized two of the swords and thrown one across the room to Will. Barbossa found himself with two swords in his hands, and suddenly his claims of honorable intentions seemed much less believable.

Sao Feng grabbed Steng and held a blade up to the pirate's face.

"Drop your weapons, or I kill your man!" he shouted.

There was a confused pause. Barbossa and Elizabeth exchanged bewildered glances. They had never seen Steng before.

"Kill him," Barbossa said with a shrug. "He's not our man."

Sao Feng could see that they were telling the truth this time. But then . . .

"If he's not with you," Will said, as though reading Sao Feng's thoughts, "and not us . . . who is he with?"

CRASH!

The answer came smashing through the windows.

East India Trading Company agents had arrived!

Chapter 4

Chaos exploded in the bathhouse. The pirates all turned to fight the East India Trading Company agents together. Whatever danger the pirates posed to each other, they knew that the agents were a much, *much*, worse threat.

Below the room, Pintel and Ragetti lit the fuses on the grenades. A moment later, an enormous explosion rocked the building, and half the floorboards collapsed, forming a ramp to the lower floor. The pirates rushed up the ramp and joined the fight.

Sao Feng shoved Steng aside and leaped into battle, leading his pirates forward. The dust from the collapsing building shrouded the fight in shadowy smoke. The clang and crash of swords and pistols rang through the darkness.

Glancing up, Elizabeth saw Beckett's aide, Mercer, striding into the bathhouse with a phalanx of soldiers behind him.

As the walls continued to tremble and collapse around them, the pirates clambered over the rubble and escaped into the street outside. Pistol shots rang out as pirates leaped from dock to dock, swung on ropes, and swarmed up ladders. They fled in all directions, fighting for their lives.

Amidst the fighting, Pintel spotted Steng and, seeing his dragon tattoo, thought that he was a fellow pirate. Suddenly, a stack of crates started to fall, and Pintel quickly leaped forward to push Steng out of the way.

Steng turned and slashed at Pintel with his knife. Pintel jumped back.

"Hey!" he protested, "you're a pirate!" But Pintel was well versed in the Code, and he knew that a true pirate would fight the East India Trading Company before his own kind—even if they were *usually* on opposite sides. This man was no pirate!

Steng grinned and slashed at Pintel again. Pintel fell backward over a rail and landed with a splash in the river below. He burst to the surface sputtering and coughing but otherwise unharmed.

A few of the agents, running through the

streets, came across the cart that Tia Dalma had been pushing. The mystic was nowhere in sight. Seeing a group of pirates turn to fire at them, the agents ducked behind the cart, using it as cover. But suddenly there was a great fluttering of wings, and all the canaries burst out through the doors of their cages, which had been left open. Something was wrong. Realizing it was a trap, the agents jumped up to run just as the cart exploded in a giant fireball.

Nearby, a wall collapsed, and Mercer was knocked into a shadowy corner. Slightly dazed, Mercer stood to rejoin the fight and then froze.

He had happened upon an interesting scene.

Sao Feng had a knife to Will Turner's throat. In the background, the sound of fighting continued. But in this dark corner, Will and Sao Feng were alone—or so they thought.

"Odd coincidence, isn't it?" Sao Feng hissed. "The East India Trading Company finds me the day you show up in Singapore."

"It is coincidence only," Will replied.

With a twist he broke free from Sao Feng's grasp. He pulled his own knife and stood facing the Pirate Lord. Unseen in the shadows, Mercer grinned and drew his pistol. Here was the perfect opportunity to kill Will Turner *and* the Pirate Lord of Singapore. He aimed carefully.

"You want to cut a deal with Beckett?" Will asked Sao Feng. "You need what I offer."

Mercer paused.

"You crossed Barbossa," Sao Feng said. "You're willing to cross Jack Sparrow—why should I expect any better?"

"They are in the way of what I want," Will said. "You're helping me get it."

Sao Feng nodded. This was logic he understood. And he stood to gain much from this underhanded deal.

"You betray me," he said in a low voice to Will, "and I will slit your throat."

"Then we have an understanding," said Will.

They lowered their knives, and Sao Feng handed Will the navigational charts to the world of the dead. With a nod, Will disappeared into the darkness, with Mercer close behind.

Having escaped the battle, Elizabeth and Barbossa ran up to the docks and found Will standing on one of the platforms. Barbossa spotted the charts in his hand.

"You have the charts!" he cried, delighted.

"And better," Will said. He indicated Tai Huang behind him. "A ship and a crew."

"Where's Sao Feng?" Elizabeth asked.

"He will cover our escape, then meet us at Shipwreck Cove," Will answered. Elizabeth was puzzled. Why had Sao Feng given in, after arguing against them so strongly? Perhaps the attack by the East India Trading Company had made him realize what a grave threat they were. Regardless, they had what they had come for, so Elizabeth decided to accept it without any further questions.

"This way," Tai Huang said. "Be quick."

Tia Dalma, Pintel, Ragetti, and Cotton appeared out of the smoke, and together they ran after Tai Huang.

From his spot in the shadows, Mercer smiled to himself. How perfect. He hardly had to do anything. The pirates were turning on each other, and as long as they were divided, they were no match for the East India Trading Company. Soon, they would be wiped out.

* * *

On board the *Hai Peng*, Will Turner stood at the rail, watching Singapore burn. The fire that had started in the bathhouse was now spreading quickly through the wooden shacks and platforms that made up the city. Although his eyes were on the flames, his thoughts were far away. Over and over, he thought about the deal he had made with Sao Feng. If only he could tell Elizabeth . . . but that was impossible. They both had secrets now. And she would never understand his motivations, just as he could not, *would* not, ever understand her feelings for Jack.

As the ship continued to sail out of the harbor, Barbossa stomped up to Will. "You weren't supposed to get caught," he snarled.

Will regarded him evenly. "It worked out the way I wanted," he said, and moved away. Barbossa could never know that Will had *deliberately* let himself be captured so he could speak privately with Sao Feng and offer a deal. It had been a risky venture, but it would be worth it if it meant he could rescue his father. He slipped down into the depths of the ship.

Elizabeth Swann stood at the rail, too, watching as the fires consumed the harbor.

"There's no place left for him to cower," she said softly. "Do you think Sao Feng will honor the call?"

Tia Dalma stepped out of the darkness. "I cannot say," the powerful mystic murmured, her eyes seeming to see beyond the burning ships and docks. "There be something on the seas that even the most staunch and bloodthirsty pirates have come to fear. . . ."

Elizabeth shivered, knowing Tia Dalma was speaking of the *Flying Dutchman*. Although it was halfway around the world, she felt as if she could sense the dreaded ship lurking in the depths of the ocean.

They had to rescue Jack Sparrow. For there was only one hope for the pirates: to stand *together* against Davy Jones and the East India Trading Company.

Chapter 5

Snow was falling.

Will reached out and caught a snowflake on his hand. Curious, he looked up at the sky and took in the dark gray clouds that were massed above them. A cold wind whistled through the sails and made all the pirates shiver.

The *Hai Peng* was sailing through a frozen landscape. They were close to the edge of the earth—in the Ice Passage between worlds. Sharp blue-and-white glaciers jutted out of the water around them, reflecting glints of pale light. The water was dark and stormy, and the snow was coming down thick and fast. At the helm, Gibbs peered into the murky grayness and steered carefully through the floating blocks of ice.

Will moved to join Tai Huang, who was leaning over the navigational charts Sao Feng had provided. They were unlike any charts Will had ever seen. Strange circles within circles moved and rotated constantly. And peculiar riddles were inscribed around the edges.

"Nothing here is set," Will said to Tai Huang, puzzled. "They can't be as accurate as modern charts."

"No," Tai Huang said enigmatically. "But they lead to more places." He walked away without explaining himself. Will watched him go, frowning. He glanced down and reread one of the inscribed poems under his breath. *"Over the edge, back, over again, sunrise sets, flash of green."*

"Barbossa," he called. Perhaps the old pirate could help. "Do you care to interpret?"

Barbossa smiled, unworried. Not bothering to answer Will, he turned toward the helm. "Ever gazed upon the green flash, Mister Gibbs?" he asked the pirate.

Gibbs nodded his head while one hand stroked his gray-flecked beard. "I reckon I've seen my share," he said. To Will, he added, "Happens on rare occasion, at the last glimpse of sunset, a green flash shoots up into the sky." He gestured into the air, keeping one hand firmly on the wheel. "Some go their whole lives and never see it. Some claim to have seen it who ain't. Some say—"

Pintel jumped in. "—it signals when a soul comes back to this world from the dead!"

Gibbs glared at him.

"Sorry," Pintel said. He slunk off to join Ragetti by the rail.

"Don't they get it?" the wooden-eyed pirate said when his friend appeared at his side. "It's a riddle. Riddles are fun! *'Over the edge, back, over again—'*"

"Riddles are not fun!" Pintel spluttered. "The way it always goes is some poor bloke ends up dead, but just beforehand he realizes no, I wasn't supposed to listen to the sirens, I wasn't supposed to take the pot o' gold, but by then it's too late, and he dies in a horrible and ofttimes ironical manner, and in this case, you and I be the poor blokes!"

His voice had gotten louder and louder as he spoke, and Will couldn't help but overhear. He turned to Barbossa with a concerned expression. Dying in a horrible and ironical manner was not part of Will's plan.

Seeing Will's expression, Barbossa laughed.

"Do not fret, Mister Turner," he said jovially. "We will find the way. It's not getting to the Land of the Dead is the problem—it's getting back!"

Will did not feel much better.

Later that night, Elizabeth once again found herself on the deck. The icy landscape was gone, the glaciers far behind them. The sea was now a dark mirror full of stars. She leaned on the rail, staring out at the water as her mind raced with unanswered questions. Would they find Jack in the Land of the Dead? Was there a way to bring him home? And . . . would he forgive her for leaving him to his death?

Jack Sparrow was a pirate through and through, Elizabeth thought. He knew that one often had to use underhanded means to get to desirable ends. He knew that she had been saving everyone else by chaining him to the mast, and he had even seemed proud of her piratelike actions. But that didn't mean he was going to be thrilled about dying. He would blame her, and she wasn't sure how he would react to seeing her again.

There was a movement behind her in the dark, and she sensed Will before she saw him. He came up and stood beside her. Leaning on the rail as well, he appeared completely wrapped up in his own thoughts, far away from Elizabeth. He seemed almost like a stranger to her. She still loved him, but she couldn't tell him about how she felt or about the guilt she was struggling with over Jack's death.

Will shifted, as if about to say something to her, but then he paused and turned away again. Elizabeth turned toward him, but he didn't look at her. After a moment, she stepped back from the rail and then walked away.

Will gazed out at the mirror of stars surrounding them, but his thoughts were not on the sight before him.

Suddenly a strange sound caught his attention. He leaned forward to listen. It sounded like . . . roaring.

"Barbossa!" he called, spinning around. "Do you hear that?"

Barbossa, standing up by the helm, cupped his hand around his ear. With a grin he said, "Aye, these be the waters I know. We're good and lost now."

"Lost?" Elizabeth repeated, alarmed.

"For certain you have to be lost to find a

place as can't be found." He winked. "Elseways everyone would know where it was, aye?" He started laughing.

Will noticed that the ship was turning on its own. It was being pulled toward the roaring sound! But Barbossa still seemed more amused than concerned.

"To stations!" Will yelled, waking the crew. "All hands! To stations!" As pirates raced onto the deck, he ran to the rigging and clambered up, trying to get a better view of what was ahead. The sound of the roaring water was getting louder and louder, and the ship seemed to be going faster.

From the rigging, Will could see a line of white foam in the distance ahead of them. The line of spray seemed to reach from one end of the horizon to the other; it stretched for miles in every direction. There was no way to get around it; they had to go back. But was it too late for that? The ship was barreling straight toward the white line, picking up speed while being dragged closer and closer.

"Rudder full!" Will shouted at the top of his lungs. "Hard a-port! Gather way and keep her trim!" If they used every sailing trick in the book, they might just escape the terrible danger ahead of them.

But as the pirates ran to obey his orders, Barbossa stepped forward and spoke in an even louder, more booming voice.

"Belay that!" he barked. "Let her run straight and true!" He seized the wheel, but Will pushed him aside and began turning it as hard and as fast as he could. The *Hai Peng* began to swing . . . but not far enough. It was impossible to fight the current pulling them toward the edge.

At the rail, Elizabeth realized with terror what was ahead of them: a waterfall. A waterfall that dropped off the edge of the world, plummeting straight down into nothingness.

Tia Dalma came up from below, an island of serenity in the chaos of panicking pirates. She tossed a set of crab claws onto the top of a barrel and leaned over them, murmuring a magical incantation.

"Malfaiteur en Tombeau, Crochir l'Esplanade, Dans l'Fond d'l'eau!" She said it again, faster, and then again, slower. As she spoke, she turned the claws in an intricate pattern, weaving them about on the top of the barrel, casting her spell. The roar of the waves was now deafening, drowning out the sound of her voice, but Tia Dalma did not

stop. She didn't even look up. Intent on the crab claws, she seemed not to care that the ship was about to plummet over the edge of the world.

Meanwhile, Will was still wrestling with the wheel, while Barbossa stood behind him, laughing. Rushing over, Elizabeth grabbed the old pirate and shook him, the spray of the water cascading around her.

"You've doomed us all," she cried.

"Don't be so unkind!" Barbossa protested. "Ye might not survive the trip . . . and these be the last friendly words ye hear. . . ." He shook his head reprovingly.

Will leaned into the wheel with all his strength. The *Hai Peng* turned, turned . . . the bow tilted away from the waterfall, but the back was dragged forward, so the ship paused for a moment, parallel to the edge. The pirates looked over the rail, down into the endless black nothingness below.

Then, with a sickening screech of timbers, the ship tilted sideways—and over the edge.

All the pirates, except Barbossa, howled with fear as the ship crashed down, down, down . . . into the inky darkness.

Chapter 6

Captain Jack Sparrow stood on the *Black Pearl*, his eyes scanning the decks. His familiar red bandana appeared even brighter in the glare of the blue sky, and the small charm that hung from his headpiece gave off a bright spark with each turn of his head.

Tilting back his tricorn hat, Jack studied the distant horizon. There was no hope of reaching it today.

"Boatswain!" he called. "Haul the halyard, slacken braces!"

Up in the rigging, another figure swung out and waved in acknowledgment.

"Aye, captain," called the man. "Slacken braces, men, make all! How does she lie?"

A sailor on deck turned around. "A fair wind and a following sea!" he cried. Then the sailor strode across the deck to Captain Jack, who was studying a knot in the ropes with a fierce expression.

Looking up at the other man, Captain Jack's scowl deepened. "What say ye about the condition of the knot on this bowline?" he demanded.

"It be proper to my eyes, sir," said the pirate.

But the captain disagreed. Within moments, they had begun to quarrel. Captain Jack's voice could be heard above the rest. His voice was rising in growing fury.

Suddenly, Captain Jack pulled out a pistol and shot one of the crew.

"You have caused us to lose speed and therefore time," the captain raved, flinging his hands into the air in exasperation. "Precious time, which cannot be recovered once lost. Do you understand?"

"Aye, captain."

"Do you now?" His eyes were wild with anger.

And they were not seeing the truth.

The sails of the *Black Pearl* hung limp. The ship's hull was half-buried in the sand of a vast, empty desert. Nothing moved in any direction. The sun beat down in a hot and merciless sky.

There was no one else on deck. Jack Sparrow was talking to himself.

Jack had not seen anyone in days, perhaps months; it might even have been years. All he ever saw now were other versions of himself. Big Jacks, tiny Jacks, but always Jacks.

He was dead and losing his mind, and he did not care for it at all.

Flapping his hands at the nearest sail, Jack blew air from his mouth. Unsurprisingly, this had no effect.

"My soul I do swear, for a breeze," Jack muttered, his gold teeth sparkling in the glare from the hot sun. "A gust. A whisper. A kiss . . ."

But there was no wind, and there hadn't been for many days.

He hoisted himself over the rail and swung down to the ground. His well-worn, knee-high boots sunk into the sand, and with effort Jack floundered over to a rope tied to the bow of the *Pearl*. He picked up the rope and leaned against it with all his strength. He strained and pulled, trying to drag the ship along the sand himself.

Of course, it was no use. The ship refused to budge.

Jack slumped down into the sand. "No wind," he said woefully.

He spotted a pile of smooth, round stones scattered on the sand near him. Picking one up, he flung it away so it skipped across the surface of the sand.

Much to his surprise, the stone stopped in midskip and came rolling back to Jack.

It paused beside his boot. Then it began rocking—back and forth, back and forth, its movements becoming faster and faster. Suddenly cracks appeared on the surface of the rock. Then, like an egg hatching, the stone split open and transformed into a small crab.

Jack stared at the crab. With an amused shake, the crab clicked its claws. Jack could have sworn it was laughing at him.

"Perfect," Jack said. "What would my torment be without unusual crabs here to mock me."

He seized a handful of sand and threw it at the crab, which scuttled backward. With a heavy sigh, Jack collapsed on his back, closed his eyes, and lay there.

His eyes closed, Jack did not see the crab inch forward. Nor did he sense the crustacean's eyes focused on him. And when, after a moment, the crab scuttled sideways to study the ship before hurrying over to the pile of stones, Jack did not notice that, either.

Time passed. Jack continued baking in the sun and drowning in despair.

Suddenly, a shadow crossed his face. With a small frown, Jack opened his eyes, blinking quickly to clear his vision.

Something was moving above him.

And that something was—the *Black Pearl*! It appeared to be floating across the sand!

Bewildered, Jack scrambled to his feet and looked his ship up and down. He bent over and peered underneath it. Then, his kohl-lined eyes widened.

The *Pearl* was not actually floating. Instead, thousands of crabs were supporting the ship on their backs. As they scuttled across the sand, they carried the *Black Pearl* along above them.

"Interesting," said Jack.

Not too far away, a different ship had met a dismal end.

Broken wreckage was scattered along the shoreline and floating in the ocean—all that was left of the *Hai Peng*.

Pintel and Ragetti floundered out of the sea first, pulling themselves onto the shore. Despite the rather desperate situation, Ragetti was grinning madly.

"What has got into you?" Pintel demanded as they collapsed on the beach.

"I thought it was fun," Ragetti said.

"It wasn't fun!" Pintel said, outraged. He scowled at Ragetti's beaming face, and then, relenting, he added, "Maybe a little, the tilting-over part—"

"And the big splash at the end!" Ragetti said with glee.

Meanwhile, other figures were beginning to appear from the waves. Elizabeth and Will swam to shore and scrambled out of the water. Gibbs and Tia Dalma were not far behind, with Cotton, Marty, Tai Huang, and the rest of his crew immediately after them. Last to emerge from the water was Barbossa, with "Jack" the Monkey clinging to his hat.

Gibbs stood on the shore and gazed up and down the shoreline. He took in the vast desert before them and the unforgiving stretch of sea behind them.

"This be truly a godforsaken place," he said darkly.

Elizabeth wrung out her sleeves and pushed her wet hair out of her face. She looked worried, too. "I don't see Jack," she said. "I don't see anyone."

"He is here," Barbossa said confidently. "Davy Jones never once gave up that which he got from the sea."

"And does it matter?" Will cried. He was furious to see all his plans going to waste. "We are trapped here, by your doing. No different than Jack." If he was now stuck in Davy Jones's Locker, there would be no way for him to rescue his father from the *Dutchman*. All of his scheming and plotting would have been for naught.

Unaware of Will's inner turmoil, Tia Dalma clucked her tongue, a mysterious smile playing at her lips. "Witty Jack be closer than you think," she said.

The others turned to look at her. Tia Dalma stared off at the desert horizon. A dozen crabs appeared from beneath the sand, scurrying up to her. She reached down to them, and they clambered up, balancing along her arms. The mystic cooed to them as if they were her pets.

Elizabeth's eyes shifted to the horizon beyond Tia Dalma. Something was moving over the dunes. She squinted, shading her eyes to see better. It looked like a sail.

It *was* a sail! More specifically, it was the *Black Pearl*'s sail!

"Slap me thrice and hand me to my momma!" Gibbs exclaimed, his eyes sparkling beneath his bushy gray eyebrows as he, too, took in the sight. "It's Jack!"

The ship rose majestically over the dunes, with Captain Jack Sparrow proudly standing at the bow, looking every inch the pirate captain again. Thousands of crabs carried the ship closer and closer to them, finally scuttling past to bring it into the water. With a splash, the *Pearl* came down, at long last back in the sea.

Will, Elizabeth, and Gibbs grinned as Jack jumped down and splashed through the water toward them. Even Barbossa cracked a smile. Jack waved to his crew, wading onto the beach.

"Will! Gibbs! Pintel and, uh, you with the one eye . . . where have you been?" he cried. "Were you killed by the Kraken? Or something else? Something painful, I hope—" Jack assumed they must be dead, like him, which would explain why they were all in Davy Jones's Locker.

Ignoring his sarcastic welcome, Elizabeth ran up to Jack and threw her arms around him, hugging him hard.

"I'm so sorry," Elizabeth said in a low voice to Jack. "So glad you're all right—"

"Contrition!" said Jack, not returning her embrace or accepting her apology. "Very becoming on you. Are you an aspect of my sun-addled brain?" He picked her up and shook her. "No." Then seeing Tia Dalma, he dropped a stunned Elizabeth and stepped forward. "Tia Dalma, out and about!" He knew that the mystic rarely left her home hidden in the swamp. "How nice of you to come! You add an agreeable sense of the macabre to any delirium—"

"How ye be, Jack Sparrow?" Barbossa's voice came from the back of the group.

Jack froze. He turned, and the crew members stepped aside to reveal Jack's old enemy, the pirate who had stolen his ship and crew, who had betrayed him and left him for dead on a deserted island. The pirate Jack had killed to regain his beloved *Pearl*.

Jack quickly forced a smile on to his face. "Barbossa!" he cried enthusiastically.

"Jack, Jack, get over here!" Barbossa responded with equal vigor.

"You old scoundrel!" Jack said, not coming any closer. "I haven't seen you in too long. Not since—"

"*Isla de Muerta*, remember?" Barbossa prompted. "You shot me!" He opened his shirt and pointed to a scar on his chest. "Right here! Lodged in my heart, it did."

Jack nodded, hiding his nervousness. "I remember," he said. "I wouldn't forget that!"

"We came to rescue you," Barbossa said. His eyes flicked to the *Black Pearl*. Noticing Barbossa's glance, Jack's expression shifted. He kept smiling, but his mind was working fast. He did not want to be indebted to this particular pirate. In fact, he did not want to be indebted to *any* of these would-be rescuers. He glanced at the ocean beside them, empty but for the *Pearl* and the wreckage of the *Hai Peng*.

"Did you now?" Jack said brightly. "How kind. But it would seem as I possess a ship and you don't, *you're* the ones in need of rescuing." He flipped his hands casually. "Not sure as I'm in the mood."

Barbossa pointed at the *Pearl*. "I see my ship right there," he said aggressively.

Jack squinted out to sea. He stood up on his toes and leaned from side to side as if searching for another ship.

"Can't spot it," he said. "Must be hiding somewhere behind the *Pearl*."

Barbossa's face turned red with anger. He could play along with Jack's games for only so long.

He stepped toward Jack as if he meant to attack him, but Will quickly intervened. It would do nobody any good for the two pirates to start fighting here.

"Jack, listen," Will said urgently. "Cutler

Beckett has the heart of Davy Jones. He controls the *Flying Dutchman*."

"He's taking over the seas," Elizabeth added.

"The song has been sung," Tia Dalma intoned. "The Brethren Court is called."

Jack snorted. "I leave you folk alone for a moment and look what happens."

"Aye, Jack," Gibbs said softly. "The world needs you back something fierce."

"And you need a crew," Will said, indicating the pirates around them.

Jack studied them with narrowed eyes. He strolled past Will, Barbossa, Pintel, Elizabeth, and Tia Dalma, eyeing them one by one. "Why should I sail with any of you?" Jack asked. "Four of you have tried to kill me in the past." He stopped in front of Elizabeth and looked her straight in the eye. "One of you succeeded."

Will started. What was Jack saying? *Elizabeth* had killed him? Jack saw Will's reaction and smiled.

"She hasn't told you?" Jack asked, amused. "Then you'll have lots to talk about while you're here." He turned to Tia Dalma and paused.

"All right, you're in." He continued down the crew. "Gibbs, you can come. Marty. Cotton, all right. And Cotton's parrot, I'm a little iffy, but all right, you're a team—" He did not bother to include Barbossa, Will, or Elizabeth.

He arrived at Tai Huang. "And you are?"

"Tai Huang," said the tall pirate with calm authority. He nodded toward the Singapore pirates who had sailed with him. "These are my men."

"Where do your allegiances lie?" Jack asked.

"With the highest bidder," Tai Huang answered.

"I have a ship," Jack offered.

"Sold," Tai Huang said.

With a satisfied nod, Jack waved to Tai Huang's men, indicating that they could board the *Black Pearl*. Pirates began splashing into the water, swimming out to the ship and swarming up the ropes to the deck.

Jack pulled out his Compass with a flourish and glanced down at it. Jack had had some trouble with the Compass in the past, when it couldn't figure out what his true desires were. But now Jack knew exactly what his desire was—he wanted nothing more than to escape Davy Jones's

Locker. He'd been wishing for an escape with all his heart for days, perhaps even weeks or months—a very long time, in any case. With his greatest desire so clear in his head, surely the Compass would point the way.

But the needle was spinning wildly. The strange realm of the dead was too mysterious for this magical object. The Compass would be no help in leading them out. Displeased, Jack snapped it closed.

"Oh, Jaaaa-ack," said a voice behind him.

Jack turned around. Barbossa held up the ancient charts they had gotten from Sao Feng. He waggled them with a toothy grin.

"Which way you going, Jack?" he teased.

Jack scowled. He had no choice. Those maps were the only chance any of them had of finding a way back to the world of the living. He would have to allow Barbossa and the others to join him on the *Pearl*.

And then they would all have to pray that the maps worked and that they wouldn't end up sailing the dark seas together . . . for the rest of eternity.

Chapter 7

The *Black Pearl's* sails billowed in the wind. Sun sparkled off the blue ocean, making the waves glisten. But underneath the waves strange dark shapes flickered, and no land could be seen in any direction. This was not the ordinary sea the pirates were used to sailing. This was the sea in Davy Jones's Locker—an endless stretch of water, where anything could happen, and the usual navigational instruments were rendered useless.

Barbossa strode about on the deck, an enormous grin on his face. At long last, he was back on the *Pearl*!

"Trim that sail!" he bellowed. "Slack windward brace and sheet! Haul that pennant line!"

"Trim that sail!" bellowed another voice behind him a half-second later. Barbossa turned and frowned at Jack, who was following close on Barbossa's heels. "Slack windward brace and sheet!" Jack hollered. "Haul that pennant line!" He puffed out his chest in an imitation of Barbossa's swagger.

"What are you doing?" Barbossa asked.

"The captain gives orders on a ship," Jack explained.

"The captain *is* giving orders," Barbossa said. He looked down his nose at Jack.

"*My* ship," Jack said, pointing to himself. "That makes *me* captain."

"They be my charts!" Barbossa shouted. The two captains were now nose-to-nose.

"Stow it, the both of you, and that's an order!" said another voice. "Understand?"

Barbossa and Jack turned slowly to see Pintel standing behind them, looking stern. They each gave him an incredulous stare, until Pintel's expression faltered, and then he put up his hands and backed away apologetically.

As Barbossa and Jack continued to bluster and argue, Will Turner stepped across the deck, searching the faces around him. He was looking for Elizabeth.

Will paced the deck, then climbed down into the cabins below. Finally he found her, sitting alone in a dark corner. Her hair was loose and her face was wet, as if she had been crying.

Will stepped into the room and stood over Elizabeth. He had not spoken to her since Jack's rescue. "You left Jack to the Kraken," he said, his heart heavy. Elizabeth's secrets went deeper than he had suspected.

Pushing back her hair, Elizabeth looked up at him. She knew he was angry and disappointed in her. But she could not feel anything but relief. They had found Jack. They were bringing him back to the world of the living. The terrible thing she had done would now be erased, and she could eventually move past the guilt, whether Jack forgave her or not. By coming here and risking everything, she had done what she had promised herself she would do.

"He's rescued now," she said wearily. "It's done with."

Will's expression remained troubled and grim. His eyes searched hers for a moment before he looked away.

Elizabeth scrambled to her feet. "Will, I had no choice!" she said.

"You chose not to tell me," Will snapped.

"I couldn't," Elizabeth said. "It wasn't your burden to bear." She started to push past him, but he pulled her around to face him.

"But I did bear it," he said, anguish in his voice. "Didn't I? I just didn't know what it was. I thought . . ."

Elizabeth looked up at him. "You thought I loved him."

She started to pull away again, but he blocked her, pushing her back against the wall of the cabin.

"If you make your choices alone," he said with quiet intensity, "how can I trust you?"

Elizabeth stopped pushing against him. She looked up into his eyes—the eyes of the man she loved, the man she had once promised to marry.

"You can't," she said softly. Will would never have been able to do what she had done to Jack. Perhaps he was too good. Perhaps she was too dark. Perhaps they were wrong for each other after all.

Will once again looked away from her, pain written across his face, the same thoughts echoing in his eyes.

There was nothing more to say. Without another word, Elizabeth ducked under his arm and disappeared from the room.

Night had fallen. It was the *Pearl*'s first night sailing the darkness between worlds. Stars glittered above and below them, and pirates moved uneasily about the deck, wondering where, exactly, the ship was going.

In the captain's cabin, two captains stood in the center of the once-pristine room. When the Kraken had attacked the ship, it had ripped apart the cabin, leaving torn papers, glass, and splinters of wood scattered around the floor. One wall was in ruins, and holes gaped out into the open air.

Barbossa kicked a pile of glass shards. "I see you neglected to care for my ship," he said.

"What, this?" Jack said. "Just ventilating. Clear out the stench of the previous owner, you know. Thinking of putting in French doors, actually. Feel the cross breeze?" He waved his hand in the air blithely, as if feeling the wind sail through.

Gibbs stuck his head through the space where the door had once been.

"Heading, Captain?" he asked.

At the word "Captain," both Barbossa and Jack spun around.

"Two degrees starboard—" Jack began.

"*I'm* captain of the starboard side!" Barbossa objected. "Two degrees starboard. The captain will now take the helm." He bolted for the door, Jack close behind.

"Aye, sirs," Gibbs said. He stood aside as Jack and Barbossa raced down the hall, up the stairs, and along either side of the ship to the wheel, where a nervous Cotton was presiding over the steering. Cotton glanced from one former captain to the other. Jack adjusted the wheel minutely. Barbossa adjusted it back. They eyed one another, both determined to prevail.

Meanwhile, Pintel was watching Ragetti. At the stern of the ship, Ragetti had been getting a fishing pole ready. Now he dropped the line over the side, peered into the dark water, and waited.

But to his horror, instead of the silvery, flickering shapes of fish, the first thing Ragetti saw in the water was the all-too-still body of a man. The body floated past, its pale face turned toward the sky, eyes closed. It was an odd sight to come across in the ocean—especially where one had been hoping to fish.

With a startled yelp, Ragetti leaped back from the railing. Curious about his friend's odder-than-usual behavior, Pintel came over to see what was going on.

There was more than one dead body.

In fact, there was a stream of bodies. Old men, young women, vigorous sailors, small children . . . the water was filled with the bodies of the dead. The two pirates strained to peer into the ghostly depths. Some of the bodies seemed closer to the surface; others floated farther down. They moved at different speeds, but all of them moved in one direction—the opposite direction from the *Pearl*.

"Downright macabre," Pintel observed.

Ragetti rubbed his chin thoughtfully. "I wonder what would happen if you dropped a cannonball on one of 'em," he mused.

They exchanged a glance. Would the flow of bodies be disrupted? Would any of them open their eyes and react? Would it sink any of the bodies it fell on?

Smiling slyly, Pintel hurried over and

grabbed a cannonball. But as he turned back, the heavy ball in his arms, he found Tia Dalma glaring sternly at him. With a start, Pintel dropped the cannonball.

"Be disrespectful, it would," he stammered.

Tia Dalma raised an eyebrow. Then she strolled to the rail and looked out at the sea, sadly watching the bodies. Even Pintel and Ragetti could tell that there was some deeper meaning here for her.

"They should be in the care of Davy Jones," Tia Dalma murmured softly, almost as if she had forgotten the two pirates were there. She sighed. "That was the duty he was charged with by the goddess Calypso: to ferry those who died at sea to the other side. And every ten years, he could come ashore to be with she who loved him truly." Tia Dalma shook her head. "But he has become a monster."

"He wasn't always all tentacley?" Ragetti asked.

"No, he was a man once," Tia Dalma said. She leaned on the rail, her faraway gaze fixed on the deep heart of the ocean. "Poor, unfortunate souls . . . now they must find their own way."

As Tia Dalma continued to gaze into the ocean, Ragetti spotted something in the darkness ahead. A small boat was floating toward them, lit by the glow of a lantern.

"Now it's boats coming," he said with surprise.

Spotting the small group at the rail, Will and Elizabeth walked over and joined them. As their eyes adjusted to the dark seas, they, too, saw boats approaching, all with their lanterns lit.

Gibbs aimed a rifle at the boats, but Will stopped him. "No," Will said. "They are not a threat to us. Am I right?"

Tia Dalma nodded. "We are but ghosts to them. They heed us not."

"Best just let them be," Barbossa said.

They all watched solemnly as the boats floated past in a silent, eerie parade. As one boat floated closer, Elizabeth started. She recognized the face.

"My father!" she cried out joyfully. "We've made it back!" She called out to him, waving frantically. "Father, here! Look here!"

Jack had joined the group, and now, looking at Elizabeth's eyes, he slowly reached out and touched her shoulder. His normally animated face was grave. "Elizabeth," he said. "We're not back yet."

Elizabeth looked up at him in confusion. Slowly realization dawned. They were the only living beings in the Land of the Dead . . . that could only mean one thing.

"Father!" she cried, her voice full of anguish. Had he died without giving her a chance to say good-bye? She should have stayed to protect him . . . what could have happened?

In the boat, the former governor of Port Royal lifted his head at the sound of his daughter's voice.

"Elizabeth!" he said, confused. "Are you dead?"

"No," Elizabeth reassured him. The man's boat was beginning to drift past, and she had to move along the rail to keep pace with him.

"I think I am," Governor Swann said reflectively.

"No," Elizabeth said. "You can't be."

"There was a chest, you see," her father said, his mind cloudy. Already he had trouble remembering the world of the living, the life he had left behind. "How odd. At the time it seemed so important."

"Come aboard!" Elizabeth insisted. She turned to the others. "Someone—cast a line! Come back with us!" she pleaded.

Crewmen moved to throw a line, but she seized it from them impatiently and cast it out herself. The end landed neatly in Swann's boat, but the governor made no move to take it or to come aboard his daughter's ship.

"And a heart," he murmured, still trying to recollect his final moments. "And if you stabbed the heart . . . you would have to sail forever. That's how it worked. Stab the heart and take his place. The *Dutchman* must have a captain. Silly thing to die for."

Elizabeth was too distraught to understand her father's ramblings, but Will and Jack both caught what he said and understood it. This was not information to let go of lightly. Jack glanced over at Tia Dalma, but she was focused on Will.

"A touch of destiny . . ." she whispered.

Governor Swann's boat was starting to drift farther and farther away. The rope between them began to slip toward the edge.

"Take the line!" Elizabeth begged again, trying desperately to save her father.

"Elizabeth," Governor Swann said, his voice suddenly clear and strong. "When I would reprimand you to obey rules, it was because I did not want you to ever be unhappy. But I should have recognized in your willfulness . . . your courage. I am proud of you, Elizabeth."

Her brown eyes swimming with tears, Elizabeth made a last urgent plea. "The line! Catch the line!"

But it was too late. The end of the rope slid out of the boat and into the water as the governor drifted out of reach.

"Father!" she sobbed. "Come back with us! Please! I won't let you go!" Elizabeth started to climb the rail and Tia Dalma spoke sharply.

"She must not leave the ship!" the mystic warned. She knew that Elizabeth would be lost to them forever if she left the safety of the *Pearl*. Will and Jack both ran to stop her, but Will got there first, wrapping his arms around her and pulling her back to the safety of the deck.

The governor waved sadly to his daughter. "I'll give your love to your mother then, shall I?"

he called as his boat was swallowed up by the darkness.

Elizabeth turned into Will's arms, pressing her tear-stained face into his chest. As Will comforted her, he looked over her shoulder at Tia Dalma.

"Is there a way?" he asked quietly.

The mystic woman shook her head. "He is at peace," she said.

Will touched Elizabeth's hair. There was nothing he could say or do for now. It would take time before Governor Swann's daughter would understand and accept her father's death. A lot of time.

Chapter 8

Daybreak came, and the sun passed slowly through the sky. It felt as if the *Pearl* had been sailing for years on this vast and empty sea. Yet, they had gotten nowhere, and there was nothing in sight in any direction.

Even the wind had fallen still. The ship drifted, the sails drooping. Worse yet, there was no water on the ship and nowhere to refill the barrels. The crew was desperately thirsty, and everyone was losing hope. Was there no way to escape these cursed waters?

Will stood at the rail, watching the sun creep down toward the horizon. Soon it would be night once again.

He saw Pintel lift a water barrel and tilt it over his head. Pintel waited, his cracked lips parted, but not a drop fell from the empty barrel.

"No water," Pintel moaned, casting the

barrel aside. "Why is all but the rum gone?"

Gibbs held up the last, empty rum bottle. "Rum's gone, too," he said.

Tia Dalma came up behind him, her eyes studying the setting sun as well. "If we cannot escape these doldrums before nightfall," the powerful mystic said, "I fear that we will sail on trackless seas, under starless skies, doomed to roam the reach between worlds . . . forever."

"With no water, forever looks to be arriving a mite soon," Gibbs added gloomily.

Will said nothing. Moving away from the rail, he went to where Sao Feng's charts were laid out on a big table near the helm. He bent over the charts once again, trying to puzzle a way out of this strange landscape. Jack was already there, studying the mysterious circles and inscriptions. In the middle, Ragetti's wooden eye rolled back and forth, an odd instrument on an even odder map.

Barbossa, meanwhile, was up by the helm, rocking on his heels. He still did not seem concerned.

"Why doesn't he do something?" Will wondered. He read the riddle once more: *"Over the edge, back, over again, sunrise sets, flash of green."*

"There's no sense to it," Gibbs said. "Sunrises don't set."

"And the green flash happens at sunset, not sunrise," Will agreed.

"Over the edge," Gibbs muttered. "Driving me bloody well over the edge."

Jack idly twisted some of the rings on the charts. As he moved them, he suddenly spotted something. When they were positioned a certain way, Chinese characters on each ring lined up to read: "UP IS DOWN."

"Up is down," Jack repeated. "That's maddeningly unhelpful. Why are these things never clear?" Suddenly a tiny Jack appeared on Captain Sparrow's left shoulder, pushing its way through his matted dreadlocks. "Stab the heart," it squeaked in his ear.

Jack jumped, very unsettled by this strange turn of events. "What?" he said.

Another miniature Jack appeared on his right shoulder. "Don't stab the heart," this one piped up.

"Come again?" said Jack. Clearly he was

83

not free of his odd visions yet. He was still trapped in the world of the dead . . . and his mind had yet to recover from the experience.

"The *Dutchman* must have a captain," observed the Jack on the right shoulder.

"That's even more than less than unhelpful," said the real Jack.

"Sail the seas for eternity," offered the Jack on the left shoulder.

"I love the sea," said Jack.

"But what about making port?" said one of the small Jacks.

"Where we can get rum," said the other. "And salty wenches. Once every ten years."

"Once every ten years," Jack mused.

"Ten years is a long time," the Jack on the left pointed out. "But eternity is longer still."

"And how will you spend it?" asked the Jack on the right. "Dead, or not?"

"Come sunset, it won't matter," answered the other. He tapped the map, watching a small drawing of a ship spin upside down. As it turned, rays spiraled out behind the ship like a sun setting.

Inspiration struck.

"Not sun-set," Jack said. "Sun-down. And

rise . . . up!" He had it! He understood the riddle!

Jack leaped to his feet. He pointed into the distance off the port side of the ship.

"Over there!" he shouted. Pirates all across the deck jumped, startled by the burst of energy. "What's that?" Jack yelled. "I don't know! What do you think?"

Gibbs rubbed his eyes. "Where?" he asked. There was nothing to see out there—just as there had been nothing to see ever since leaving the beach where they had found Jack.

Jack ran over to the railing, and everybody followed him, crowding around to stare in the same direction.

Suddenly, Jack turned and raced across to the starboard side.

"There, it moved!" he called as he ran. "It's very fast!"

The others chased after him, and the ship tilted as their weight shifted to the other side. Meanwhile, Elizabeth had been huddled by the rail, lost in her own sadness thinking of her father. But as the ship started to tilt farther over, her attention was finally captured. She looked up in time to see Jack whirl around again.

"Thar! Over thar!" Jack shouted, running back to port with everyone running after him. Now even Elizabeth stood up and followed. The ship tilted even further back to the port side.

"What is it?" Elizabeth asked.

"It's not here!" cried Jack.

Once more he ran to the starboard side, and once more all the pirates ran after him, and once more the ship tilted even more.

Curious, Barbossa approached the table with the charts. He saw the message reading UP IS DOWN. He saw the drawing of the upside-down ship and the rays of the sunset.

"He's rocking the ship," Pintel observed, bewildered.

"We're rocking the ship!" Gibbs agreed, running with all the others.

All at once, Barbossa understood what Jack was up to.

"Aye, he's on to it!" Barbossa cried. "All hands together! Time it with the swell!"

The former captain of the *Pearl* ran over to the hold and cupped his hands to bellow down to the men belowdecks.

"Loose the cannon!" he called. "Unstow the cargo! Let it shift!"

Pirates ran to follow his orders. Crates were cut loose from their moorings. Barrels and bottles rolled freely across the floor, clattering from side to side as the ship continued to tilt more and more.

Cotton spun the wheel to turn the ship sideways to the swell. The waves helped the swing of the ship's tilt.

"He's rocking the ship!" Pintel exclaimed again, only this time he understood why. As the pieces fell into place, Ragetti ran up to him with a long rope.

"We tie each other to the mast," Ragetti explained, "upside down, so we'll be right side up when the boat flips!"

Pintel couldn't completely follow this logic, but it sounded all right to him. He quickly lashed Ragetti to the mast.

Meanwhile, Will raced to the rail with the others, gazing out across the empty ocean at the horizon, where the sun was sinking rapidly into the sea. The last rays began to disappear below the waves . . . the *Black Pearl* tilted back in the other direction . . . and Jack shouted: "And now, up is down!"

With an enormous heave, the ship overturned completely, sending everyone and everything under the water.

The sails billowed as water filled them. Chains, cannons, cannonballs, and anything not tied down plummeted into the depths. Pirates clung to the rails; Jack, Barbossa, Will, and Elizabeth held on tightly to the ship. Gibbs lost his grip and began to float away, but Marty caught him and pulled him back. Pintel and Ragetti, tied to the mast, held their breath.

Will saw the charts begin to float away, and he reached out with one hand to grab them.

Then suddenly . . .

A flash of green on the horizon!

And *THWUMP!*

Water cascaded away from the *Black Pearl* with a giant splash. Everything came crashing back down onto the deck: pirates, cannons, parrot, and all.

The *Pearl* was floating on the surface of the sea once again. But this was not the cold and empty sea of the underworld. Here, it was sunrise.

Daylight was spreading across the sky, and an island beckoned from the near distance.

They had escaped Davy Jones's Locker. They were back in the real world at last.

Chapter 9

Jack immediately checked his hand. No Black Spot—did that mean his debt to Davy Jones was paid? Was Jack finally free of the Kraken's chase? He took a deep breath, savoring the fresh air of the world of the living.

"Blessed sweet westerlies!" Gibbs exclaimed, staring about them. "We're back!"

Pintel and Ragetti opened their eyes. They were still tied to the mast—upside down.

"This was your idea," Pintel said. "And the fact that I went along does not make you any less stupid."

"Well, it don't make you no more smart, neither," Ragetti retorted.

Will ignored the quarreling duo and turned, his eyes searching the deck. He found Elizabeth standing by the rail, gazing at the horizon. Cautiously, he made his way over.

"It's a sunrise," she said, with a smile. They weren't safe yet—Davy Jones and Lord Beckett were still out there. But they had rescued Jack Sparrow and escaped the world of the dead. Reason enough to stop and celebrate.

Barbossa and Jack were grinning, too. A ripple of pleased relaxation spread across the deck, and then . . .

Quick as a wink, everyone drew their pistols and pointed them at each other.

Barbossa's pistol was pointed at Jack, and so was Elizabeth's. Will and Gibbs had their pistols trained on Barbossa. Jack aimed his pistol at Will; he quickly drew another and aimed it at Barbossa. Barbossa, too, pulled out a second pistol, which he pointed at Gibbs, while Elizabeth pointed her second pistol at Barbossa.

In the midst of everything, Pintel and Ragetti worked frantically to get themselves free.

Despite the unnerving fact that he had four pistols aimed in his direction, Barbossa did not seem particularly worried. Glancing from weapon to weapon, he smiled.

"All right, then," he said, taking a deep breath. He had been prepared for this moment.

He knew getting Jack out of Davy Jones's Locker was going to be the easier of his tasks. Now he had to set about the harder task—convincing Jack to attend the meeting of the Brethren Court. The wily captain would not be eager to go—many of the Pirate Lords would not be pleased to see him again. But it was the only way to make the sea safe for all pirates once more. Captain Jack Sparrow simply had to attend.

And *that* meant everyone had to work together. Barbossa continued, "The Brethren Court is a-gathering at Shipwreck Cove. Jack, you and I be going there, and there's no arguing the point."

"I am arguing the point," Jack objected. "If there's pirates a-gathering, I'm a-pointing my ship the other a-way."

"The pirates are gathering to fight Beckett," Elizabeth said, jumping into the conversation. "And you're a pirate." She took her second pistol off Barbossa and pointed it at Jack. In return, Jack stopped aiming at Will and aimed at her instead. But Elizabeth stared him down. She was not about to give up. Lord Beckett was a menace and a murderer. The East India Trading Company was a scourge to the seas. They had to be stopped.

From his spot on the deck, Will pulled out a second pistol, so he now could aim at Jack *and* Barbossa.

"Fight or not, you're not running," said Will.

"If we don't stand together, they'll hunt us down, one by one, 'til there's none left but you," Barbossa said.

They all knew it was true. Lord Cutler Beckett would be happy with nothing less than the complete annihilation of *all* pirates.

Jack grinned. "Then I'll be the *last*. At least then there will be only one of me."

"Then you'll be fighting Jones alone," Barbossa said. "How does that figure into your plans?"

"Still working on it," Jack admitted. "But I'm not going back to the Locker, Barbossa. Count on that."

He cocked the pistol that was pointed at Barbossa. Then he fired.

Click.

Barbossa, Will, and Elizabeth all fired as well.

Click. Click. Click.

Nothing happened. No gunshot, no puff of smoke. They studied their pistols, puzzled. Gibbs shook his and checked the barrel.

"Wet powder," he explained.

Will sighed and tossed his useless pistol aside. "So for now we're in this together," he said. "Right now, we need water. The charts show an island nearby." He pointed to a spot on the map, and then off at the small piece of land in the distance. "There. With a freshwater spring. We can resupply, and then get on with shooting each other." It was a sensible plan. They could all agree about needing water more than anything else.

Jack eyed Barbossa suspiciously. "You lead the shore party," he said. "I'll stay with the ship."

"I'll not be leaving *my* ship in your command," Barbossa scoffed.

"And he'll not be leaving his ship in your command," Will interrupted. "Here's an idea. You both go, and leave the ship in *my* command."

Barbossa and Jack looked horrified and indignant at the very thought of Will captaining their ship.

"*Temporarily,*" Will added. "All right?"

Uneasily, the two men agreed. Everyone else let out a relieved sigh. They had a plan—and a temporary peace.

A short time later, several longboats neared the deserted shore, while back on the *Black Pearl*, Elizabeth, Will, Tai Huang, and a small contingent of pirates waited uneasily. From his spot at the front of one of the boats, Jack could see something large lying down the beach. While his eyes grew wide, his mouth remained shut.

The landing party leaped into the surf and pulled the boats up on the beach. Pintel and Ragetti, who had finally managed to free themselves of the mast, floundered through the waves. Suddenly, Pintel noticed the thing Jack had seen.

"Criminy!" he exclaimed.

Jack and Barbossa climbed out of the boats, and together, all the pirates walked cautiously along the sand toward the object. It looked like a giant whale.

A few steps closer, and all the men knew exactly what it was.

It was the Kraken!

The gigantic sea monster lay dead on the beach. Its tentacles were splayed out, its enormous eyes staring at nothing.

Jack Sparrow's most feared nightmare, the creature that had chased him across the Seven Seas and finally killed him, was now dead, while *he* had returned to the living.

Unsure of how to react, Jack moved even closer, approaching the creature with something like awe.

Pintel found a stick of driftwood lying nearby. Picking it up, he poked the Kraken, jumping back quickly just in case.

"Careful!" Ragetti said.

"Ahh, not so tough now, are you?" Pintel jeered. "Stupid fish! Serves you right!"

"Hello! I bet folk would pay a shilling to see this!" said Ragetti. "And a second shilling for a sketch of 'em sitting atop!"

"Kraken slayers!" Pintel said with glee. "We could carve mini'ture krakens out of coconut and sell those, too! We could give 'em a slice as a souvenir!"

Ignoring the pirates' inane banter, Jack stepped closer to the Kraken. If he hadn't seen it with his own two eyes, he would not have believed it. It was almost . . . sad. As far as he knew, the Kraken had been the last of its kind. And here it lay, alone, nothing but a pile of rubbery tentacles where there had once been an awesome monster.

"Still thinking of running, Jack?" Barbossa said softly from behind him. "Think you can out-run the world? The problem of being the last of anything: by and by, there be none left at all."

"Sometimes things come back," Jack said. "We're living proof, mate."

"Aye, but that's a gamble with long odds, ain't it?" Barbossa answered. "There's no guarantee of coming back. But passing on—that's dead certain."

Jack considered that for a long moment. He didn't want to think about his own death right now, so soon after having escaped the first one.

"The world used to be a bigger place," Barbossa said.

"It's still the same size," Jack answered softly. "There's just less in it." He sighed heavily. It seemed he had no choice. "Summoning the Brethren Court, is it?"

"Our only hope."

"That's sad commentary, in and of itself," Jack said softly.

Moments later, the landing party climbed up to the freshwater spring, ducking through under-growth and weaving around palm trees. The spring bubbled up from the ground into a clear pool surrounded by sharp rocks and black sand.

Despite his short stature, Marty was the first to reach the well. As he eagerly stooped down to drink, he noticed something floating in the pool. He leaned forward to take a closer look—and then jumped back with a horrified cry.

There was a dead body in the water.

Barbossa brought a handful of the water to his mouth, tasted it, and spat it right back out.

"Poisoned," he stated. "Fouled by the body."

Two of the pirates crouched down and turned the body face up. Barbossa was shocked to realize that he recognized the dead man. It was Steng—the East India Trading Company agent who had posed as one of Sao Feng's pirates back in Singapore! A wooden fid, like the spike Sao Feng had threatened Will with, was driven through one eye.

A terrible suspicion gripped Barbossa. Almost immediately, as if in answer to his fears, a shout came from the direction of the beach. The pirates all rushed back to the shore to find Ragetti pointing frantically out to sea.

The *Black Pearl* was no longer alone in the water. Another ship was floating beside her. Barbossa quickly recognized the Chinese fighting ship. It was Sao Feng's *Empress*.

An ominous click sounded from behind them. Jack and Barbossa turned to find Tai Huang and his men training pistols on them. Unlike their own waterlogged weapons, they knew that these pistols would actually fire. And Tai Huang's pirates would not hesitate to use them.

Both men let out a heavy sigh. Luck was not on their side.

They had been betrayed.

Chapter 10

As the landing party was escorted back onboard the *Pearl*, Barbossa and Jack could see that the pirates loyal to them had been shackled and stripped of their weapons. A swarm of Chinese pirates had taken over the ship, far too many to fight.

But at least one person had tried to resist. Elizabeth Swann stood chained between two guards who showed the unfortunate aftereffects of trying to fight her. One had a bloody lip; the other had an eye that was swelling up. Neither looked pleased.

At almost the exact same moment, Barbossa and Jack spotted Sao Feng. Still dressed in the dark robe he had donned in Singapore, the Pirate Lord cut a striking figure against the blue sky. His eyes calm and his expression smug, he now strolled across the deck toward them.

"Sao Feng," Barbossa said, narrowing his eyes. "You showing up here, 'tis truly a remarkable coincidence."

"Fortune smiles upon those prepared to meet its gaze," Sao Feng answered wisely. He moved closer to Jack, who had quietly slid behind Barbossa and was now trying—unsuccessfully— to be as inconspicuous as possible. "Jack Sparrow. You paid me great insult, once."

Without warning, he punched Jack in the face, sending the pirate's hat flying. Jack staggered back and nearly fell, but, flailing his arms, he managed to stay on his feet. He bent over and picked up his hat, putting it back on his head.

"So now we can call it square," Jack said, his eyebrows rising in hope.

"Hardly," Sao Feng spat.

At that moment, Will appeared from belowdecks, looking anxious. He quickly took in Jack's bruised jaw and Barbossa's angry glare. Then he saw Elizabeth in chains and hurried over to Sao Feng.

"She's not part of the bargain," Will said. "Release her."

"And what bargain be that?" Barbossa said sharply.

"You heard Captain Turner," Sao Feng said to his men, a hint of mockery in his voice. "Release her."

"*Captain* Turner?" Jack cried indignantly. How could this upstart whelp be a captain on Jack's own ship?

"Aye," Gibbs said with a gloomy air. "The perfidious rotter led a mutiny against us."

The weathered first mate was right. With the help of Sao Feng's pirates, Will had over-thrown Jack's crew and taken over the *Pearl*. Now he planned to take the ship to find the *Dutchman* and rescue his father.

Jack shook his head. "It's always the quiet ones," he muttered.

As the chains dropped away, Elizabeth rubbed her wrists and stared at Will, her expression pained. She would never have guessed that he could betray them all like that.

"Why didn't you tell me you were planning this?" she asked.

"It was my burden to bear," said Will, echoing her own words back at her. Elizabeth frowned and stood up straighter. If Will had confided in her, perhaps she could have helped him find another way. As it was, he was playing a very dangerous game, trusting all their lives to Sao Feng and his men.

"The only way a pirate can make a profit these days is by betraying other pirates," Barbossa said, repeating the words Sao Feng had said back in Singapore. Unfortunately for Barbossa, they had taken on a darker meaning as *he* was now the one betrayed.

"I can live with that," Sao Feng replied, "as long as I am not the other pirates."

"But you've no acrimony toward mutineers?" asked Jack. Jack himself had plenty of acrimony, now that he'd been mutinied against . . . twice.

"He did not mutiny against *me*, did he?" Sao Feng pointed out. No one had ever dared mutiny against the powerful Pirate Lord of Singapore.

"I need the *Pearl*," Will said. "That's the only reason I came on this voyage."

"He needs the *Pearl*," Jack said, pointing at Will. Then he turned to Elizabeth. "And you felt guilty." He pointed at Barbossa. "And you and your Brethren Court . . . didn't anyone come to save me just because they missed me?"

Gibbs, Marty, and Cotton raised their hands. A moment later, Pintel and Ragetti raised their hands as well. And so did "Jack" the Monkey.

Jack moved toward his loyal crew. "I'm standing over there with them."

But before he could get very far, Sao Feng grabbed his arm. "I'm sorry, Jack," he said, not sounding very sorry at all. "But there's an old friend who wants to see you first."

"I'm not certain I can survive any more visits from old friends," Jack said nervously, rubbing his jaw where Sao Feng had punched him.

"Here is our chance to find out," Sao Feng said slyly.

He pointed over Jack's shoulder, and Jack turned to see a very unwelcome sight rounding the island. It was Lord Cutler Beckett's ship, the *Endeavour*. Jack stifled a groan. He had managed to elude the East India Trading Company for a long time . . . but no longer. He was trapped.

Chapter 11

Jack Sparrow had found himself in his fair share of sticky situations. Now it appeared he was in yet another one.

After being unceremoniously dragged away by Sao Feng's guards, he found himself thrown into the captain's cabin of the *Endeavour*. Lord Cutler Beckett, his white wig perfectly coifed, stood at the window, staring out at the sea.

The guards dropped all of Jack's things on the table, including his Compass. With a brief nod, Lord Beckett dismissed the guards, leaving him alone with Jack. He remained at the window, his eyes now trained on the *Pearl*, as Jack glanced around the room.

"Remarkable," Beckett mused. "When last I saw that ship, it was on fire and sinking beneath the waves. I fully expected that to be the last I saw of it."

As he spoke, Jack began to tiptoe around the room, peeking into cabinets and boxes.

"Close your eyes and pretend it's all a bad dream," Jack said flippantly. "That's how I get by."

"You can stop searching, Jack," Beckett said, still without turning around. "It's not here."

Jack froze, then carefully replaced the lid on the jar he'd been peering into.

"'It' being what?" he asked casually.

Beckett turned around then, fixing Jack with a knowing look. "Understand what it is a man wants," he said, "and no amount of knavery and machination makes him any less predictable." Jack still looked confused. "The heart of Davy Jones," Beckett explained. "It's not here. It's safely ensconced aboard the *Flying Dutchman* and therefore unavailable for use as leverage to satisfy your debt to the good captain."

Jack paused to consider Beckett's news. So the heart wasn't here—but at least he now knew where it was. That, in and of itself, was far more than he had hoped to learn when dragged on to the *Endeavour*. But as for the debt . . . "By my reckoning, that account's been settled," Jack said.

"By your death," Beckett agreed. "And yet, here you are."

Jack considered this and then shrugged. "Yes, here I am," he said. "Painfully aware I am, in fact. Why am I?"

Beckett stepped over to the table and picked up Jack's Compass. He hefted the weight of it in his hands for a moment, then held it up for Jack to see.

"You've brought me this," he said. "I owe you a pardon and a commission." Beckett smiled thinly. He remembered all too clearly the bargain he had struck with Will Turner, although it seemed like a lifetime ago. When he had released Will from prison to search for Jack, he had offered a pardon for Jack in exchange for his Compass. And Beckett was always a man of his word. . . .

"So I am offering you a job," Beckett said to Jack. "In the employ of the East India Trading Company. Working for me." His smile grew wider. He loved the idea of having Jack Sparrow under his boot. Forced to work for the very Company he hated—the Company that aimed to destroy everything that pirates stood for! It was quite the brilliant revenge.

But Jack was not so eager to bargain. He tilted his head and made a tsk-tsking noise. "We've been down that road before, haven't we?" he said. "And we both know how you get when your advances are spurned." He held up his wrist, where the burn of a branding iron had left its mark.

Beckett's face went cold with anger. Sparrow was impossible. "I had contracted you to deliver cargo on my behalf," he said, trying to keep the anger out of his voice. "You chose to liberate it."

"People aren't cargo, mate," Jack said.

Beckett shook his head. "You haven't changed," he said. "Our business is concluded. Enjoy the gallows."

"I've been," Jack said flippantly. "Once you've taken in the view, there's not much else to it." His voice shifted, becoming more serious. "But the fact is, I *have* changed. If you'll entertain for a moment a counterproposal." He produced a piece of eight from a hidden pocket and rolled it meaningfully between his fingers. "The Brethren Court."

Beckett pulled out his own piece of eight and imitated Jack's gesture, scoffing.

"I am already aware of the Brethren Court and that it is meeting," he sneered.

"But you don't know where, do you?" said Jack. "I do." He flipped the coin onto the table, where it spun in a circle for a moment. Beckett watched the coin, as if hypnotized.

"That's the offer on the table," Jack said. "You square things with Jones on my behalf, assure me of my freedom, and in exchange . . ." Jack Sparrow smiled. "I will lead you to Shipwreck Cove and deliver up all the Pirate Lords on a silver platter."

Back aboard the *Black Pearl*, things were not going quite the way Will had expected. The ship was already full of Sao Feng's pirates, and as he watched, a crew of sailors from the *Endeavour* came aboard as well. They were led by Beckett's aide, Mercer. It was he who had arranged a deal between Sao Feng and the East India Trading Company after overhearing the Pirate Lord's secret conversation with Will back in Singapore. The very same deal that was now due to be completed.

Quickly, Mercer's men began to spread out across the ship, taking positions and preparing to sail. As Sao Feng and Will watched, one of the men took the wheel from Tai Huang. Will glanced at Sao Feng in confusion. This was not part of *their* deal.

"My men are crew enough," Sao Feng objected, apparently confused as well.

"Company ship, Company crew," Mercer said with an oily smile.

"You agreed," Will said, turning to Sao Feng. "The *Black Pearl* was to be mine."

"And so it was," Sao Feng said. He gestured to one of his crew, who punched Will from behind, knocking the wind out of him. Will collapsed to the deck, gasping, as two other men shackled his arms.

Sao Feng turned to Mercer, his betrayal of Will neatly taken care of. "Lord Beckett agreed," he said, "the *Black Pearl* was to be *mine*."

Mercer smiled again. "And so it was," he echoed. Sao Feng stiffened. He could see now that he was going to be betrayed in turn. Shaking his head, Mercer added, "Lord Beckett wouldn't give up the one ship as might prove a match for the *Dutchman*, would he?"

The Pirate Lord looked around at the East India Trading Company men, all of them armed. They outnumbered his own men and looked ready

Can Captain Jack Sparrow survive Davy Jones's Locker?

Elizabeth Swann and Barbossa arrive in Singapore.

Will Turner has been caught stealing.

Sao Feng does not want to help save Jack Sparrow.

Davy Jones and his encrusted crew are killing pirates everywhere!

Lord Cutler Beckett is pleased. He possesses Davy Jones's heart.

Barbossa must convince Jack to travel to Shipwreck Island.

Tia Dalma tells Will they must return to the
land of the living by sunset.

Jack's crew wants to help their captain.

Elizabeth Swann is worried about Will and
the fate of pirates everywhere.

Will Turner and Lord Beckett arrive for Parlay.

Can the two sides agree or will there be war?

to fight. If he started a battle here, there was every chance he could lose—and then he'd lose his deal with Lord Beckett as well. He'd be back to being another pirate in their sights . . . a pirate they would hunt down and kill without mercy.

With a sharp nod, he stepped back, and so did his man at the wheel, turning control over to Mercer. It pained Sao Feng to give up so easily, but he didn't see any other choice. Mercer gave Sao Feng a mocking half-salute and strolled away.

As Sao Feng stood fuming, Barbossa sidled up beside him.

"Shame they're not bound to honor the Code of the Brethren," Barbossa murmured. "Isn't it? Of course, honor's a hard thing to come by, nowadays."

"There is no honor to remaining with the losing side," Sao Feng responded sharply. "Leaving it for the winning side . . . that's just good business."

"The losing side, says *you*," Barbossa observed.

"They have the *Dutchman*," Sao Feng said. "And what do the Brethren have?" Nothing that could fight such a powerful ship, he was sure. And yet . . . if they did . . .

Barbossa leaned in closer. "We have . . . Calypso."

Sao Feng's eyes widened in surprise. Every pirate worth his salt had heard of the ancient sea goddess. Everyone knew the stories of how she had once ruled the ocean with her powerful magic. And every Pirate Lord could tell the tale of the very first Brethren Court, when the nine original Pirate Lords had captured and bound Calypso in human form. They had used a magic even more ancient than her own, taming her wild fury and bringing the sea under their command.

But surely those were just stories. Surely there wasn't a real Calypso—an actual goddess, trapped as a human. Or was there? Sao Feng's eyes darted across the ship toward the one woman on deck—Elizabeth. Barbossa did not fail to notice.

"Calypso," Sao Feng said hesitantly. "An old legend."

"No," said Barbossa, his voice growing thick. "The goddess herself, bound in human form . . . fury or favor, you not be knowing . . . but when the mood strikes her, and its her favor she bestows upon a lucky sailor . . . well, you've heard—legendary."

Sao Feng had heard the tales. In the old days, when she was still powerful, if Calypso took a liking to a man of the sea, everything would go his way. The lucky captain who won her love would find only fair weather and smooth seas. He could easily be master of the ocean with the help of a goddess like her.

"There was a time when the seas be untamed, the world a rougher place, and a sailor made his own fate," Barbossa continued. He paused, letting his words sink in. Then he leaned toward Sao Feng again. "I aim to bring it back," he said. "And for that, I need the Brethren Court." With a significant look, he added, "All the Court."

"What are you proposing?" Sao Feng said quietly.

"What be you accepting?" Barbossa asked, suspecting he knew the answer already.

Sao Feng nodded across the ship. "The girl," he said.

Barbossa smiled. His fellow Pirate Lord had fallen for his plan.

From where she stood, Elizabeth had not

been following the conversation. But now, feeling the men's eyes on her, she looked over.

The conversation had caught Will's attention as well. "We give you Elizabeth in exchange for helping us escape?" he asked, horrified.

Sao Feng nodded.

"No," Barbossa said, pretending to care for Elizabeth's safety. "No. Out of the question."

"It was not a question," Sao Feng said.

"Done," said Elizabeth.

The others gaped.

"What?" Will cried out. "Not done!"

"You've put us in these straits," Elizabeth said to him, her anger finally spilling over. "If this frees us, then . . . done." She lifted her chin and stared bravely at Sao Feng.

"No," Will protested, his heart breaking. He had lost the *Pearl* and his one chance to rescue his father. Did he now have to lose his one true love as well?

"My choice," Elizabeth insisted. "My choice alone."

"Elizabeth, they are pirates," Will said.

She gave him a scathing look. "I've had more than enough experience dealing with pirates," she said. Her meaning was clear . . . pirates like *you*. She couldn't trust him any more than any other pirate . . . probably less so than many, in fact.

Sao Feng smiled broadly. "I am pleased—" he began, reaching out to take her arm. Elizabeth yanked it away. She had agreed to go with him, but nothing else. To her surprise, he held up his hands and bowed respectfully. "My apologies," he said. "I know I must earn your favor."

Elizabeth didn't know what he meant by that, but she squared her shoulders and tried to look regal. "That's right," she said. "You do."

"Then we have an accord?" Barbossa asked.

"Agreed," Sao Feng said, shaking Barbossa's hand. He would tell his men to fight the East India Trading Company sailors and steal the *Pearl* back for Barbossa and for Jack's men. He would help them to convene the Brethren Court.

In exchange, Elizabeth would sail away with him on the *Empress*.

Chapter 12

Meanwhile, in the captain's cabin of the *Endeavour*, Jack Sparrow paced back and forth, his hands gesturing wildly. He was outlining the terms of an agreement between himself and Lord Beckett.

Through narrow and guarded eyes, Beckett took in the scene. He had learned from past experience to be wary of any plans that came from the peculiar, and often devious, mind of Jack Sparrow.

"You can have Barbossa," Jack said, counting on his fingers. "The belligerent homunculus and his friend with the wooden eye, both. And Turner. Especially Turner."

Beckett tapped his fingers together, noticing who Jack did *not* mention. "And what becomes of Miss Swann?" he asked.

"The rest go with me aboard the *Pearl*,"

Jack answered, "and I will lead you to Shipwreck Cove. Do we have an accord?"

Lord Beckett smiled at Jack's outstretched hand. But he did not shake it. Instead, he ran his fingers over the objects on the table and picked up the Compass again. "Jack," he said, "remember, I have this wonderful Compass that points to whatever I want."

"Points to what you want *most*," Jack noted. "And that's not the Brethren Court, is it?"

"No?" Beckett asked. "Then what is, Jack?"

"Me," said Jack. "Dead."

Beckett stared at him. Jack waved toward the Compass and gave a small bow, as if to say "try it." Beckett flipped open the Compass and looked down at the needle. Sure enough, it was pointing directly at Jack. Beckett scowled.

Jack did a small sideways dance, and the needle followed him across the cabin.

Curse Jack Sparrow! He was right. What Beckett wanted most in the world was to see Sparrow dead.

Which meant the Compass was utterly useless to him. He threw it back at Jack, who caught it neatly in his hands. Beckett could wait. Jack could be useful for a short while, and then he could be just as dead later on, after the Pirate Lords were all captured.

Or . . . there was another option. Beckett raised his head. "It occurs: if I got what I wanted most, then wouldn't what I wanted second most become the thing I wanted most?" He took an ominous step toward Jack. "With you dead, I can find . . . Shipwreck Cove, was it? On my own." He took another step, his face dark. "Cut out the middleman, as it were . . . literally."

Jack stepped back and began talking quickly. "Then you'll arrive at the cove, find it's a stronghold, nigh impregnable, able to withstand blockade for years, and you'll be wishing, wishing, if only there was someone *inside* to ensure the pirates come *outside*."

Beckett paused and thought for a moment. "And you can accomplish this?"

"I'm Captain Jack Sparrow, mate," Jack said, puffing up his chest. "Do we have an accord?" He stuck out his hand again. Beckett hesitated.

Suddenly, the ship was rocked by a huge explosion. Beckett stumbled forward, and Jack grabbed his hand, shaking it vigorously.

"Done!" Jack cried. He grabbed the rest of his things off the table and ran for the door as cannon fire continued to shake the *Endeavour*, blasting the wooden sides with fierce volleys. Beckett followed close behind.

Up on deck, Jack and Beckett found themselves staring at chaos. Bodies were littered across the deck, and smoke rose from the cannon ports below.

On the horizon, they could see the *Empress* sailing away, while gunshots and blasts of cannon fire still came from the nearby *Pearl*.

Jack was not going to watch his ship sail away—again. He glanced around, looking for a way to get himself over to the *Pearl*. His eyes widened, and he ran over to one of the cannons. Shoving the gunner away, he quickly flipped the cannon over so it was facing toward the *Pearl*. Before Beckett could even react, Jack had wrapped a rope around the cannon wheel, a burning fuse lighter in his hand.

"You're mad!" Beckett exclaimed.

"Thank goodness for that," Jack said. "Or else this would never work." He leaned back and lit the cannon.

Beckett and his crew dove out of the way as the cannon fired, sending an enormous cannonball hurtling seaward, the force causing it to glance off the *Endeavour*'s mast. Dragging behind came Jack, hanging on to the rope for dear life.

On board the *Pearl*, Barbossa saw Jack come flying through the air toward them. He couldn't believe it. Typical Jack. True, he was escaping, but he was doing it in the most dangerous and foolhardy way possible.

Barbossa winced as a series of horrible crashing sounds signaled Jack's arrival. He peeked his eyes open again to see a path of destruction across the deck: a splintered barrel, a ripped sail, scattered gunpowder. And then, standing on the rail, looking completely relaxed and unhurt—Jack Sparrow himself.

"Tell me you didn't miss me!" Jack cried, grinning.

Hopping down from the rail, he spotted Will among the crew. "Send this traitor to the brig," he commanded. Jack's crew set upon Will at once, shackling him and dragging him down to be imprisoned in the depths of the ship.

Jack beamed. All was as it should be. He was back on *his* ship. Just how he liked it.

Meanwhile, back on the *Endeavour*, Lord Beckett was standing amidst the wreckage, fuming. This was decidedly how he *did not* like it. An officer by the name of Groves came up to him looking for orders.

"Which ship do we follow?" he asked, his face pale and ashen.

"Signal the *Dutchman*," Beckett said. "We follow the *Pearl*." He glanced up at the mast, which had cracked from the impact of Jack's cannonball. "How soon can we have the ship ready to pursue?"

As if in answer, the mast cracked a bit more and then snapped in two, crashing down with the sails billowing out behind it. Beckett knew the *Endeavour* would not be ready to sail again for quite some time. Jack Sparrow had seen to that.

Groves stared after the *Pearl* in admiration, shaking his head. "Do you think he plans it all out," he asked, "or just makes it up as he goes along?"

Chapter 13

Elizabeth Swann was not unused to privilege. After all, she was the daughter of a governor. But what she was not used to was luxury *among pirates*.

Aboard the *Empress*, Elizabeth now found herself surrounded by opulence and beauty. A strange combination in the heart of a pirate's world and one that caught Elizabeth unawares— neatly putting her at Sao Feng's mercy.

The Pirate Lord's cabin was lit by flickering candlelight, which cast a glow over the shimmering hanging silks and the soft pillows scattered around the floor and on couches. Deep reds and golds added a level of exotic warmth to the cabin.

The room was not the only thing decorated. When she had first stepped on the ship, three Chinese maidens had attended to her every need. They had bathed her and dressed her in a traditional Chinese gown made of soft, shining silk.

Now she stood in the middle of the beautiful room waiting for Sao Feng . . . waiting to find out what he wanted from her.

The Pirate Lord entered the room quietly and for a moment stood still, amazed by the vision before him. Elizabeth's eyes sparkled with fire, and her skin glowed in the dim lamplight. The simple Chinese gown she wore made her appear both utterly female and utterly powerful. She looked like . . . a goddess.

Stepping forward, Sao Feng began to recite a verse from the poem "To Zhang's Dancing": *"Young willow shoots. Touching, brushing, the water. Of the garden pool,"* he said.

He picked up a decanter from a low table and offered Elizabeth a glass of wine. She accepted it uncertainly.

"I admit," she said, "this is not how I expected to be treated." She had thought she would be a prisoner, perhaps punished for her role in stealing Sao Feng's charts or for getting him into such a mess with the East India Trading Company.

Sao Feng smiled over the rim of his glass. "No other treatment would be worthy of you . . . Calypso."

Elizabeth froze with the glass at her lips. What was he talking about? "Excuse me?" she said. Was he treating her so well due to some kind of mistaken identity? If so, it probably wouldn't be wise to let him know he was wrong.

"Not the name you fancy, I imagine," Sao Feng said, "out of the many that you have . . . but it is what we call you."

"We being who?" Elizabeth asked.

"Whom," Sao Feng corrected her.

"Who," Elizabeth insisted.

He considered the correction for a moment, and then shrugged, moving on. "We of the Brethren Court and our predecessors, who concealed you in this form. Your forgiveness. I lied. Who *imprisoned* you—oh. 'Who.' You were right." He looked impressed, but Elizabeth was more concerned with the story than her grammatical win.

"Goddess?" she asked.

"You confirm it?" Sao Feng said quickly.

"Confirm what?" Elizabeth asked. "You've told me nothing." She moved to sit on the low red couch, trying to conceal just how little she understood of the situation. Sao Feng followed her.

"The Brethren Court—not I, the first Brethren Court, who . . . whom . . . *whose* decision I would have opposed," stammered Sao Feng. "They bound you in human form, so that the rule of the seas would belong to men, and not . . ."

"Me," Elizabeth said, beginning to understand.

"But one such as you should never be anything less than what you are," Sao Feng said charmingly.

"Pretty speech from a captor," Elizabeth said, tossing her head and causing the extravagant headpiece she wore to slip a bit. She leaned back on the crimson silk and attempted to appear calm. "But words whispered through prison bars lose their charm."

"Can I be blamed for my efforts?" Sao Feng asked, leaning forward. "All men are drawn to the sea. Perilous though it may be." He gazed into her eyes, and she knew he wasn't talking only about the sea.

"Some men offer desire as justification for their crimes," she said softly.

"I offer simply my desire," he answered.

A small smile crossed her lips. "An item of such small value," she teased. "And in return?"

"I would have your gifts, should you choose to give them."

Yes, it was very clear now. Sao Feng had been sorely mistaken. She was not who he thought, nor did she have the powers he needed.

"And if I choose not?" she said, lifting her chin.

"Then I will take your fury," Sao Feng said. He took her shoulders and kissed her.

Surprised, Elizabeth pushed him away. But before she could do or say more, she heard a muffled explosion in the distance.

They both looked up, just as a cannonball blasted into the hull with an enormous crash, sending splinters of wood flying everywhere. Up on deck, there were shouts and screams and the sounds of pirates running to battle stations, pistols blazing. Elizabeth took cover behind a couch as more lead balls slammed into the room. Outside the porthole, the night was dark, and all she could see were fire and flashes of explosions. She had no way of knowing *who* was attacking.

Another explosion rocked the ship. Elizabeth crawled to her feet and spotted Sao Feng through the smoke. He was lying on the floor, a long, sharp shard of wood buried in his chest, blood pooling on the boards around him.

"Sao Feng?" she cried.

"Here," he gasped. "Please."

He fumbled at his neck, pulling off the rope-knot pendant he always wore. "The Captain's Knot," he murmured. "Take it. So you'll be free! Take it! I must pass it on to the next Brethren Lord."

"Me?" Elizabeth exclaimed, astonished.

"Go in my place to Shipwreck Cove," he said.

"Captain!" a new voice yelled from the hallway. Tai Huang burst through the door, the sound of fighting close behind him. "The ship is taken!" Tai Huang cried. "We cannot—" He stopped short, seeing Elizabeth leaning over Sao Feng. The Pirate Lord whispered something in her ear, the life draining out of him.

"Calypso," Sao Feng murmured, his eyes closing. With one last sigh, he died in Elizabeth's arms. She slowly lowered Sao Feng's body to the deck, then stood up and turned to Tai Huang, her expression grave but resolute.

"What did he tell you?" the Pirate Lord's lieutenant asked.

She held up the rope-knot pendant.

"He made me captain," she said.

Chapter 14

The new captain of the *Empress* stepped out onto the deck, where bodies lay motionless and cannon smoke drifted through the air along with the moans of wounded pirates. Following close behind her came Tai Huang.

Elizabeth frowned as she finally caught sight of the ship that had attacked them.

It was the *Flying Dutchman*.

The barnacle-encrusted crewmen were swarming up onto the *Empress*, rounding up terrified sailors and shackling them. Elizabeth did not see Davy Jones among them, but suddenly the smoke parted, and she saw someone else she knew striding through it.

It was Admiral James Norrington—a man she had once been betrothed to, but whom she had never wanted to marry. She knew it was he who had stolen the heart of Davy Jones and handed it over to Lord Beckett. In exchange, he had regained his place in the Royal Navy and was a respectable officer once more. In her eyes, however, he had become less respectable for doing so.

"James?" she said cautiously.

Norrington's eyes widened when he saw her. Of all the people he had expected to find on the ship of the Pirate Lord of Singapore, Elizabeth was certainly not among them.

"Elizabeth!" he cried. Joyfully, he embraced her.

"I heard you were dead!" he said, taking her shoulders and looking her up and down. He didn't dare believe his eyes. But there was no denying it. This was definitely Elizabeth Swann, alive and well despite what Davy Jones had told Governor Swann. "Your father will be overjoyed to know you are well," he said.

"My father is dead," Elizabeth told him.

"No, he's not," Norrington said innocently. "He returned to England."

Elizabeth's expression was scornful. "Lord Beckett told you that?"

Norrington paused. "Yes," he said, but

hesitantly. Should he trust Beckett's word—over Elizabeth's?

At that very moment, Davy Jones himself arrived on deck and began to inspect a line of trembling sailors. His tentacles twitched and writhed as he eyed the men.

"Who among you do you name as captain?" he barked.

Tai Huang pointed at Elizabeth. Norrington could not have been more surprised if *he* had been named captain himself. Elizabeth Swann, captain of a Chinese warship? Was it possible?

Despite the evil presence of Jones, Elizabeth stood straight and tall. Her eyes were cold and betrayed not a hint of the emotion Norrington knew she must be feeling. There was no question the woman standing in front of him was no longer the refined governor's daughter—she was a pirate captain through and through.

"Tow the ship," Norrington said, turning his attention back to his own crew. "Take the sailors to the brig."

"You heard the admiral!" Davy Jones called.

"The captain may have my quarters," Norrington added, with a low bow to Elizabeth.

"No, thank you, sir," Elizabeth said proudly. "I prefer to remain with my crew."

She moved to follow her fellow pirates, who were being led away to the brig on the *Dutchman*. Norrington stopped her, his eyes pleading.

"Elizabeth, I swear, I did not know," he said.

"Know what?" she replied, her voice laced with scorn. "Which side you chose? Now you do."

In the depths of the *Dutchman*, crew members from the *Empress* were locked in different cells. Elizabeth stepped through into the cold space and flinched as the door clanged shut behind her. She turned to look at the sailor who had escorted her in—a strange-looking man with a rough complexion like coral.

Suddenly, she remembered something. Will's father, Bootstrap Bill, was a crewman on the *Dutchman*. If she could find him, maybe he could help them escape.

"Bootstrap?" she asked the sailor who had locked her in.

The man just cackled and walked away. Either it wasn't him, or he wasn't going to help. A short way down the passage, a barnacle-covered seaman was mopping the floor. Elizabeth pressed her face to the bars and called softly: "Bootstrap? Bill Turner?"

She got nothing but a grunt in response. With a sigh, Elizabeth slumped down with her back against the wall. It was no use. She couldn't go searching for Will's father—she was trapped in this cell. She'd have to wait and try the next crewman who went past.

Suddenly, a pair of eyes opened in the hull next to her.

"You know my name!" croaked a voice.

Elizabeth jumped and scrambled away. She stared at the hull in shock. There was a man embedded in the wood of the ship! He was barely human anymore. Only his face seemed capable of movement.

But this must be Bill Turner, Will's father. She felt a pang of sadness for Will, that his father had been reduced to such an existence.

"I know your son," she said gently. "Will Turner."

Bootstrap's face lit up. "William! He's all right?" he asked. Elizabeth nodded. She thought it kindest to leave out the fact that at that very moment, his son was probably locked up in the *Pearl's* brig.

"He made it!" Bootstrap said in a wondering voice. "He's alive. Hah! And now he's sent you to tell me that he's coming to get me. He promised. God's wounds, he's on his way!"

Elizabeth's heart ached for the poor man, and for Will. She knew that Will had only tried to steal the *Pearl* because he was desperate to save his father. But now, looking at what had become of Bootstrap, she knew it had all been for naught. There was no way to save the man. He was but wood and sea life now . . . hardly anything of Bootstrap himself was left.

"Yes," she said aloud, trying to sound encouraging. "Will is alive, and—he wants to help you." That much was true. She couldn't exactly say that he was on his way, but if he could be, she knew he would.

But it was too late. The hope was fading from Bootstrap's eyes. A look of despair crept across his face instead. "No," Bootstrap muttered. "He can't come. He won't come."

"I don't know how," Elizabeth admitted, "but he will try, I am sure. You're . . . his father."

Bootstrap studied her with sad eyes. "I know you," the old pirate said. "He spoke of you. Elizabeth."

"Yes," Elizabeth said, a little surprised that he remembered her name.

"He can't save me," Bootstrap said. "He won't. Because of you."

"Me?"

"You're Elizabeth," he said.

There was a long pause before Bootstrap snapped back to attention. "If Jones be slain," he said, "he who slays him takes his place. Captain. Forever." Seeing the look of horror on her face, he added, "Every man before the mast knows that, Elizabeth! The *Dutchman* must have a captain."

"I see—" Elizabeth said, finally understanding.

"If he saves me . . . he loses you."

"Yes," she said quietly.

"He won't pick me," Bootstrap said shrewdly. "*I* wouldn't pick me. The *Dutchman* must have a captain."

"You said that," Elizabeth pointed out. His words were starting to blur together, as if he were losing his train of thought.

Bootstrap nodded, and his features began to fade back into the hull of the ship. His voice grew fainter as he said, "Tell him—don't come! Tell him—stay away! Can you tell him? It's too late. I'm part of the ship. The crew."

His eyes closed, and he went still. Now he looked just like a carving, a wooden extension of the ship. The man Will knew as his father was no more—and he could no more help Elizabeth escape than the walls or the boards of the ship could. Now Elizabeth would have to bear the news in silence.

Chapter 15

In another part of the ocean, not too far away, the *Endeavour*'s repairs were finally done, and the ship was in pursuit of the *Black Pearl*. Lord Beckett stood on deck staring out to sea, as Greitzer, one of his lieutenants, scanned the horizon with a spyglass.

Suddenly Beckett spotted movement in the far distance. He squinted and then turned to the lieutenant.

"Glass," he demanded curtly.

Greitzer handed over the spyglass, and Beckett peered through it.

Strangely, the movement seemed to consist of a flock of birds congregating around something floating on the water.

Beckett ordered the ship to head in that direction.

As the *Endeavour* drew closer, the birds' cries

grew louder and louder. The tower of birds stretched up into the sky, and their wings flapped as they circled and dove toward the floating object.

It was a dead body. Beckett's lip curled when he saw that it was one of his own men. The bloated, pale shape had been lashed to two barrels to insure that it floated. This was no accident. This man had not merely been tossed overboard; he had been left floating . . . as a sign.

Beckett ordered the body hauled onto the deck, although he daintily stayed out of the way of the corpse. Further investigation revealed a rum bottle on the man with a note inside.

It bore the symbol of the East India Trading Company.

Beckett smiled.

"Sir," interrupted Greitzer, pointing at the distant horizon. Nearly out of sight but still visible was another tower of circling birds. Someone was most definitely leaving a trail for them . . . a path leading straight to the *Black Pearl*.

"Like bread crumbs," Beckett mused. "Ghastly." He indicated the note. "And we are meant to follow. Adjust course, Lieutenant."

* * *

Night had fallen. On board the *Pearl*, a shadowy figure crouched by the rail, tying another dead body to a barrel. With a heave, he began to lift it up to push it overboard.

But then a voice spoke up from behind him, freezing him in place.

"I knew the brig wouldn't hold you," said Jack.

Will Turner dropped the body and whirled around. He reached for his sword, but Jack flapped his hands casually.

"Hold on, William," he said. "Do you notice anything? Or, rather, do you not notice anything? Or, rather, do you notice something that is not there to be noticed?"

Will blinked, sorting through the jumbled series of questions. "You haven't raised an alarm," he said.

"That's odd, isn't it?" said Jack. He studied the body and the barrel that Will had been lashing together. "But not so odd as this."

"I'm leaving a trail," Will admitted. "For Beckett."

"And you came up with this plan yourself?" Jack asked.

Will nodded uncertainly.

Jack was impressed, despite himself. It was a high-quality plan, full of piratey backstabbing and skulduggery. Not the typical style for young Mr. Turner.

"Hmm," Jack said. "What do you intend to do, once you've given up the location of the Brethren?"

"Ask Beckett to free my father."

Jack snorted. "Now, *that* sounds like a plan you'd come up with. You couldn't trust Beckett to keep that bargain even if you shook on it; he certainly won't if you've already given him what he wants." He scrutinized Will. "You know what it will take."

"Killing Jones," Will admitted with a sigh.

"And you know the cost," Jack said. "Conveying the spirits of those that died at sea, not stepping foot on land but once every ten years . . ."

Will slumped. He knew it was all true. He knew that saving his father meant condemning himself to an immortal lifetime as the *Dutchman's* captain. He knew that it meant he could never be with Elizabeth.

"I'm losing her, Jack," Will said unhappily. "Every step I make for my father . . . is a step away from Elizabeth."

For so long, all he had wanted was her affection. For ten years he had waited for a sign that she could care for him. And then Jack arrived, and despite the rather dramatic adventure that followed, it had been worth it. Elizabeth had opened her heart. And now all of that felt so terribly far away. Then, he remembered the man standing beside him. In a low voice, he added, "She was willing to do anything to save you."

"From the fate she consigned me," Jack pointed out.

"She felt terrible about killing you," Will countered.

"Yes, she's a prize, that one," Jack said, rolling his eyes. Studying Will, a thought came to mind. Perhaps he could make all of this work to *his* advantage. "What if there was a way to avoid making the choice at all?" he asked, his eyes gleaming. "Were someone else to dispatch Jones . . . that would free your father, just as sure as if you had done it yourself."

"Who?" Will asked, confused.

Jack cocked his head. When Will still didn't get it, Jack spread his arms and made a *"tada!"* gesture.

"You?" Will said with immense surprise. "Last I knew, you were desperate to *avoid* service aboard the *Dutchman*."

Jack shrugged. "Death has a way of reshuffling one's priorities," he observed. "I know what awaits me in the world beyond this one. It is not a place I intend to revisit—ever." Besides, he knew, being captain on the *Dutchman* would be quite a different story from serving *under* Davy Jones.

Jack Sparrow leaned forward, his excitement growing as his plan took shape. "I get aboard the *Dutchman*," he outlined eagerly, "I find the chest, I stab the beating thing. Your father goes free from his debt, you are free to be with your charming murderess, and I am free to sail the seas forever." He grinned. It really was a rather fantastic plan.

"You'll have to perform Jones's duty," Will pointed out, not quite as taken by the idea.

"So not quite free, then . . . but immortal has to count for something."

Will rubbed his head, debating. Sparrow

was far from the most reliable of allies. Still . . .

"How can I trust you, Jack?" he asked.

"Trust is an elusive thing," Jack said, "but he needs must go when the devil drives, eh?" He pushed something into Will's hands. Will glanced down and saw Jack's famous Compass. Jack continued, "Here. Be sure to give Davy Jones my regards."

Will looked up again, puzzled, but his expression quickly turned to surprise as Jack shoved him over the side of the ship.

With a huge splash, Will landed in the water. A moment later, the barrel and the body lashed to it splashed down right beside him. Will paddled over and clung to the barrel.

From above, Jack leaned over the rail with a broad smile. He waved cheerfully and disappeared.

Will sighed. As usual, Jack was following his own plan, and Will had no choice but to go along with it. Around him, the dark water slapped the barrel, while above, a pale moon barely cut through the clouds.

It was going to be a very long night.

Chapter 16

On another part of the ocean, Elizabeth Swann found herself in darkness, too. Hers, however, was quite a bit drier. She was curled in a corner of a cell in the *Dutchman*'s brig. The barnacled ship sailed smoothly through calm seas, towing the *Empress* behind it.

Suddenly she heard the scrape of metal against metal. Her eyes flew open, and she saw her jail door slowly opening. Was it one of the *Dutchman*'s crew? She shuddered at the thought of one of the part-ocean-creature sailors creeping into her cell in the dark.

But then a lantern flickered in the darkness, and Elizabeth recognized the voice of James Norrington.

"Be quiet," he whispered. "This way. Hurry." He beckoned urgently.

Elizabeth scrambled to her feet and saw

that her crew members had been freed as well. They looked to her for guidance, and she nodded. Silently, they crept, scurrying toward the deck on catlike feet.

"What are you doing?" Elizabeth whispered to Norrington.

He met her eyes. "Choosing a side," he answered.

She gazed back at him, then nodded. He led the way along the passage, Elizabeth following closely. Behind them, the cell door hung open.

And inside the cell . . . a pair of eyes opened in the hull of the ship. Bootstrap Bill saw the open door and the now empty cell. With great effort, he detached himself from the wood, stepping forward. His mind cloudy, he shuffled out and along the passage to the deck.

Up on the stern balcony, Norrington led the way to the towrope that connected the *Dutchman* to the *Empress*. Elizabeth's crew immediately knew what they had to do. One by one, they slung themselves over the edge and began to crawl along the line. Hand over hand, they pulled themselves back to their own ship.

"Quickly now," Norrington whispered. He

turned to Elizabeth. "Do not go to Shipwreck Cove," he urged. "Beckett knows of the meeting of the Brethren. I fear there is a traitor among them."

Elizabeth shook her head, her eyes sad. "It is too late to earn my forgiveness," she said.

"I do not ask it," Norrington said. "I had nothing to do with your father's death. But that does not absolve me of my other sins." He knew there was no way to redeem himself for his mistakes, even though he had only been trying to be a good soldier. He only wished he could make Elizabeth understand—through it all his love for her had never wavered, despite her rather unfortunate inclination toward the pirate life.

Staring at the man before her, Elizabeth saw the regret and emotion in his eyes. Finally, she believed him. She saw that he meant what he said; that he knew what he had done, and that he was sorry for it.

"Come with us," she said impulsively.

Norrington hesitated.

"James. Come with me," Elizabeth said, taking his hand. Norrington was torn. He wanted very much to go with her although it went against his nature as a member of the Royal Navy . . . but so did letting them escape in the first place. He was sure to be in grave trouble once his treachery was discovered. And he had chosen Elizabeth's side . . . the pirates' side . . . perhaps he *should* go with her. . . .

He glanced at the line of Chinese sailors swinging across to their ship. Nearly all of them had made it now.

"Who goes there?" a voice said suddenly from the darkness. A figure shuffled toward them.

Norrington whirled and drew his sword. The moment was broken. He knew where he had to stand; where he would always stand.

"Go!" he cried to her. "I will follow."

"You're lying," Elizabeth said. She knew him well enough to know that. Norrington looked into her eyes. "Our destinies have been entwined, Elizabeth," he said, "but never joined." Impulsively, he took her in his arms and kissed her. Only for a moment—and then he pushed her back toward the rope.

"Go! Now!" he shouted.

Unwillingly, Elizabeth stepped over the rail and took the rope. She was the captain of the

Empress now. Her crew needed her. But James might need her, too. With one last look over her shoulder, Elizabeth began to shimmy out across the open water. She could only hope that Norrington would follow shortly.

Meanwhile, on the *Dutchman*, the shuffling figure had stepped into the circle of light cast by the lantern. It was Bootstrap Bill.

The old pirate wasn't sure what was going on. His mind was fuzzy and dim, with vague thoughts and memories flitting through it. Through the fog of confusion, his eyes made out a recognizable figure—Elizabeth, his son's beloved. She was crawling away along a towrope. A small part of his brain nagged at him. He knew that wasn't right. The crew of the *Dutchman* stayed with the *Dutchman* forever.

"No one leaves the ship," Bootstrap said.

"Stand down," Norrington said. "That's an order."

"Part of the crew," Bootstrap mumbled. "Part of the ship."

Norrington quickly realized that this was no ordinary sailor. This one was much further gone than the others; he'd become so much a part of the ship that he'd begun to lose his true self. That made him unpredictable.

"Steady, man," Norrington said, trying to make his voice sound soothing and calm.

But it was too late. "All hands!" Bootstrap bellowed in a surprisingly loud voice. "All hands! Prisoner escape, all hands!"

Crewmen quickly appeared from all directions, racing across the deck.

Elizabeth was halfway across the rope, but she heard the commotion and looked back. She saw the *Dutchman*'s sailors descending on Norrington.

"James!" she cried. She couldn't leave him in such a dire situation. She started to crawl back to the *Dutchman*.

But Norrington saw what she was doing, drew his pistol, and fired through the towline. It snapped apart, sending the free rope swinging back to the *Empress* and splashing Elizabeth into the water.

As Norrington spun back to face the approaching crewmen, Bootstrap lurched forward. His faltering brain dimly remembered his purpose as a pirate—defend the ship at all costs.

He drew his cutlass and stabbed Norrington through the heart.

The admiral cried out just as Elizabeth emerged, sputtering, from the water and dragged herself up the rope to her ship, hand over hand. Dangling by the Empress's hull, she looked back at the *Dutchman* as the ships sailed apart.

"No!" she cried in horror. "James!"

But it was too late. Norrington collapsed to the deck, dying. Bootstrap stood over him, still holding his bloody sword, uncertain of what he had done or what was happening.

There was nothing Elizabeth could do. The *Empress* sped away into the dark, leaving the *Dutchman*—and the dead body of James Norrington—in her wake.

A ripple of shock spread through the *Dutchman's* crew. "The Admiral's dead!" one of them cried. "The Admiral's dead!" Did this mean the marines were no longer in charge of the ship? Could Davy Jones and his crew retake control?

In high excitement, the crewmen raced to the captain's cabin, where the heart of Davy Jones was being held prisoner. They burst through the doors—only to find a troop of terrified soldiers standing with their rifles pointed directly at the heart.

Behind them stood Beckett's aide, Mercer. His eyes were steely, and his expression was severe. He tilted a small cannon into place, pointed squarely at the chest.

The crew came to a halt, subdued.

"Nothing has changed," Mercer said with calm authority.

Jones watched, his gaze full of cold hatred, as Mercer relocked the chest and hung the key around his neck. There would be no mutiny here. The heart—and the *Dutchman*—were still firmly under the foot of the East India Trading Company.

Chapter 17

While the *Empress* was pulling farther away from danger, the *Black Pearl* was drawing ever closer to it.

In the middle of a vast, empty sea floated a strangely shaped island: Shipwreck Island. It was hollow, with a round water cove in the center. It was here the Brethren Court would meet.

The *Black Pearl* was fast approaching the island. Gibbs stood behind Cotton at the wheel, intently watching the seas.

"Look alive, and keep a careful eye!" he instructed Cotton. "Not for nothing it's called Shipwreck Island, where lies Shipwreck Cove and Shipwreck City!"

Jack tilted back his hat and looked over at them. "You know," he said, "for all that pirates are clever clogs capable of the most under-handed and duplicitous thinking . . . we are an unimaginative lot when it comes to naming things."

"Aye," Gibbs agreed.

"Step out, Mister Cotton," said Jack, moving to take the wheel himself. "There's some dangerous cross tides ahead that will prove a trick to navigate."

On the forward deck, Barbossa stood lost in thought. The culmination of a complex plan was at hand, and there was still much at risk. A rustle behind him signaled the approach of someone, and he turned to see the powerful mystic, Tia Dalma, watching him intently.

"Barbossa," she hissed in a low voice, "why you not giving the order to man the guns? All the Brethren be gathered in this place. You can force them to do as you want!"

"What I want," Barbossa said calmly, "is not to act the fool, and what you're suggesting is naught but fool's folly."

Tia Dalma stepped closer to him, caressing his cheek.

"If you no longer want my favor, Barbossa," she crooned, "then perhaps I should be calling a different captain to my cause." Her gaze slid across the deck to the man at the wheel. "Witty Jack would not turn down the promise to survive the coming storm, I think."

Barbossa sniffed, unconcerned. "I do not renege on a bargain once struck," he said, "but we agreed to ends only; the means are mine to decide."

With a hiss of anger, Tia Dalma caught Barbossa's wrist in a fierce grip. She squeezed, and cold magic trickled through his veins. Before his eyes, Barbossa saw his hand decay, turning skeletal and dead.

"Caution, Barbossa," Tia Dalma said. "Do not forget it was by my power you be returned from the dead . . . or what it means if you fail me."

She released his arm and the flesh and color slowly returned to it. But as she began to move away, he caught her arm and pulled her close to him, his own voice trembling with fury.

"And don't you forget," he whispered, "why you had to bring me back, and why I could not leave Jack to his well-deserved fate, and why I could not give Sao Feng a second smile in his throat to match that ineffably smug one he wears on his face." He gestured toward Shipwreck Cove.

"It took nine Pirate Lords to bind you, Calypso—and it takes no less than nine to set you free. 'Til then, I'll not be taking commands from you, nor risk you reaching accord with someone else!"

He looked up and caught the attention of some nearby pirates. "Mr. Pintel! Mr. Ragetti!" The two crewmen snapped to attention. Barbossa shoved Tia Dalma—Calypso, the ancient sea goddess, once so powerful, now trapped in human form—in their direction. "Take this . . . fishwife to the brig!" he ordered.

Pintel and Ragetti seized the mystic and escorted her away, but Barbossa could feel her furious glare burning into his back as she was dragged belowdecks. He couldn't worry about that now. Once he convened the Court . . . once he tricked the Pirate Lords and performed the spell to set her free . . . then she would surely forgive him anything. She would show him her favor, and he would be the greatest pirate on the seas, and all would be well.

Until then, he just had to keep her locked up so she couldn't ruin his plans.

Dusk was falling as the *Pearl* sailed straight toward

a towering cliff face. Pirates gathered along the rail, looking worried. Surely Jack was sailing them right into the rocks.

But at the last moment, they came around a giant rock formation and spied a hidden sea tunnel in the rocks ahead of them. The crew breathed a sigh of relief.

Slowly the ship maneuvered through the tunnel, toward a light burning in the distance. At long last, they emerged from the rocky channel into a wide cove, surrounded on all sides by towering cliff walls. In the center was Shipwreck City, a town constructed entirely of broken, derelict ships all loosely connected to each other. From a distance, it looked to be naught but flotsam, jetsam, and debris. It seemed impossible that amidst the wreckage, there could be a meeting place worthy of the Brethren Court. However, there was something rather majestic about the island—as though it, like pirates themselves, was far more powerful than appearances would have one believe.

Moored around the island were a host of various pirate ships from all over the world. The other Pirate Lords had already arrived.

Pintel and Ragetti stared out, astonished.

"Look at them all!" Pintel exclaimed.

"There's not been a gathering like this in our lifetime," Barbossa said, looking pleased with himself.

Jack sighed. "And I owe all of them money."

Meanwhile, some distance away, Will had been found and dragged aboard the *Endeavour*. He now stood soaking wet and manacled, unsure of what would happen next. Lord Beckett's ship and the *Dutchman* were moored alongside each other as Beckett planned his next move. Davy Jones had been summoned to the deck of the *Endeavour*, much to his extreme displeasure.

"I believe you know each other," Beckett said to Davy Jones, gesturing to Will.

Jones smirked. "Come to risk your luck against me again, have you?" he asked, referring to their previous encounter, when Will bested him at a game of Liar's Dice.

"No," Will said. "To join you. Well, him." He nodded at Beckett.

"Tell him what you told me," Lord Beckett said.

Will took a deep breath. The manacles weighed heavily on his hands, and he was tired from a long night drifting at sea and fighting off birds who had found him as tempting as the dead body beside him. But he had a mission, and he would see it through. "Barbossa has summoned the Brethren Court for a purpose. To free someone named Calypso."

Jones stiffened, a new look twisting his features—fear. Lord Beckett nodded, as if he had expected that.

"Calypso," Beckett repeated significantly.

"No," Jones said. "They can't. The Heathen Gods care for nothing and no one but themselves, and she is the worst of them. The Brethren were to keep her imprisoned forever; that was the agreement."

Will gave him a scrutinizing look, some of the pieces of the puzzle coming together. "*You* told the first court how to bind her," he realized. "And that's why you cut out your heart—"

Jones slammed his claw down on the table. "*Do not* venture there." He turned to Beckett. "We must stop them," he said urgently. "She will destroy us all."

Lord Beckett nodded slowly, looking thoughtful. "It is more imperative than ever that we find the Brethren Court," he said. "Which presents a problem." He turned to Will. "With you here, *if* it was indeed you who left us the trail—"

"It was," Will insisted.

"—then how will we find them now?" Beckett finished.

"I want your assurances," Will said, trying not to let his anxiety show in his voice. He needed to sound calm and in control of the situation. "Elizabeth will not be harmed."

"Ah," Beckett said. "Elizabeth. Of course." He paused before answering. "The last I knew of Miss Swann, she was captain of the *Empress*."

"Captive," Will corrected him automatically.

"No, captain," Beckett repeated.

Will thought about that for a moment, puzzled. "Nonetheless," Will said, shaking off the troublesome questions, "she will not be harmed." He turned to Davy Jones. "And my father goes free."

"You ask much," Jones said, his tentacles writhing.

"I offer much," Will pointed out. He knew

that this was his only chance to bargain with them.

"Where is Shipwreck Cove?" Lord Beckett hissed.

"I don't know," Will said.

Jones darted forward, pressing the tip of his claw into Will's chest, and snarling into his face as the tentacles of his beard snaked around Will's neck.

"Then you have nothing we want!" he growled viciously.

But Jones was wrong.

Will looked at Beckett and held up . . . Jack's Compass.

"What is it you want most?" he asked with a smile.

Chapter 18

BOOM! BOOM! BOOM!

The loud sound rang through the chamber of the Brethren Court as Barbossa hammered on the tabletop with a cannonball.

Jack glanced nervously around the room. He had a lot of enemies in here.

The chamber was hidden in the abandoned hull of a derelict ship, with curved spars rising up on either side of them like the ribs of a long-dead prehistoric beast. In the center of the candlelit room was a large oval table. Eight Pirate Lords were assembled around it, some alone, others guarded by attendants.

Eight swords, one for each Pirate Lord who had arrived, were stabbed into a globe nearby, where the pirates had left them before taking their seats. In theory, this was supposed to be a peaceful gathering . . . in practice, it would be astonishing for Jack Sparrow to escape this room alive.

Lining the walls behind the Lords were their crews, packing the room full of fierce—and fully armed—pirates. While all of them had felt the threat from the East India Trading Company—they'd all had skirmishes with each other in the past, too. Feelings of trust were not running high.

Barbossa continued to bang on the table until silence finally descended upon the room. "As he who issued summons, I convene this, the fourth Brethren Court," he declared. He gestured to a wooden bowl lined with a red scarf, in the center of the table. "Your Pieces of Eight, my fellow captains."

Grudgingly, each Pirate Lord stood and dropped an item into the wooden bowl. Pintel, perched on a ledge and peering over the heads of the assembled pirates, noticed that the objects weren't actually silver pieces of eight—they were odds and ends of things one might find on any pirate ship—or in any busy harbor.

"Those aren't pieces of eight," Pintel objected to Gibbs. "Those are just pieces of junk."

Gibbs nodded. "The original plan was to use coins," he explained, "but when it came time, the first Pirate Lords didn't have a pence between them. But everyone liked 'Nine Pieces of Eight,' so the name kind of stuck."

This didn't make a lot of sense to Pintel, but then again, he wasn't a Pirate Lord, so what did he know?

Barbossa held out his hand. "Mr. Ragetti, if you will?"

"I kept it safe," said Pintel's friend, "like you said when you gave it to me."

"Aye, you have," said Barbossa, "but now I need it back." When the pirate still hesitated, Barbossa leaned over and gave him a slap on the back of the head. Ragetti's wooden eye popped out, dropping into Barbossa's outstretched hand. Ragetti pulled out an eye patch and slipped it on as the Pirate Lord tossed the eye into the bowl.

Apart from Barbossa, Jack, and the missing Pirate Lord, there were six pirates gathered around the table. Ammand the Corsair was a tall, black-haired pirate who was known as the scourge of the Barbary Coast. Beside him sat Villanueva, a taciturn Spaniard with a bad temper. Captain Chevalle was next, an aristocratic Frenchman with a sneering expression, elegantly attired in brocade with lace cuffs. Fourth was Gentleman Jocard, a former slave turned pirate, whose gleaming black skin and fearsome muscles attracted many stares.

Then there was Mistress Ching, a female Chinese pirate. She was the only woman . . . but, she was nonetheless one of the most dangerous people in the chamber.

And finally there was Sri Sumbhajee, a serene pirate who had traveled from the Indian Ocean for this meeting. He looked like an innocent, benevolent priest, but he was flanked by two hulking, nasty-looking bodyguards named Akshay and Pusan. He was not a man to upset.

As the Pieces of Eight clattered into the bowl, Mistress Ching lifted her head. "We're missing two," she said alertly.

Villanueva turned and glowered at Jack. "Sparrow," he growled.

Jack cocked his head, considering. If he handed over his Piece of Eight, there would be no more need for him here. Who knew what the others might do to him once they had it. Pirates, were, after all, quite the vengeful lot.

"We're still short one Pirate Lord," Jack pointed out. "I'm content to wait until Sao Feng joins us."

"Sao Feng is dead," said a voice from the doorway.

Everyone turned to see Elizabeth Swann in full pirate garb, and Tai Huang and another Chinese crewman standing behind her. Jack's mouth dropped open in surprise.

"Before he died, he named me captain of the *Empress*," Elizabeth explained, "and passed his lordship on to me."

She started forward, but Tai Huang touched her shoulder to stop her and pointed toward the globe. Elizabeth drew her sword and stabbed it in alongside those of the other Pirate Lords.

"Captain?" Jack squawked indignantly. "*Captain*? They're just *giving* the title away now!"

"By whose hand did he perish?" demanded Ammand the Corsair.

"Hers I wager," Jack muttered.

"Will you never forgive me?" Elizabeth said to him. Then she turned to answer the

Pirate Lords. "He fell to the *Flying Dutchman*."

The room erupted in chaos at the mention of the terrible ship.

Jack and Elizabeth could see alarm spreading on the faces of the Pirate Lords.

"*Le monster des profondeures!*" Chevalle cried in dismay. The pirates along the edge were shouting in horror, demanding that they take to the seas and escape before the *Dutchman* found them.

"Listen!" Elizabeth yelled. "Listen to me! Our location has been betrayed! Jones, under the command of Lord Beckett—they are on their way here!"

This news, of course, only led to further uproar.

"And who is this betrayer?" Gentleman Jocard snarled, as if he were ready to strangle the traitor with his bare hands.

"Not likely anyone among us," Barbossa said pointedly.

Elizabeth looked around, and something occurred to her. "Where's Will?" she asked Jack.

"Not *among us*," Jack answered.

Barbossa hammered on the table again,

calling for quiet. "It does not matter how they found us!" he cried. "The question is, what will we do now that they have?"

"We fight," Elizabeth said in a voice that sounded stronger and braver than she felt.

Pirates all around the room began laughing. Fight the *Flying Dutchman*? Was she crazy? Did she think they were all fools, to throw their lives away so easily?

Mistress Ching stood and spread her hands, offering another option. "Shipwreck Cove is a fortress, a well-supplied fortress," she pointed out. "There is no need to fight, if they cannot get to us."

A murmur of agreement rippled across the chamber. That was true. They could hide for a long time here, wait until the *Dutchman* and the East India Trading Company gave up and left them alone.

"There is a third course," Barbossa said. The room fell silent as everyone turned to look at him. He paused, waiting until he had their full attention. "In another age," he began, "at this very spot, the first Brethren Court captured the sea goddess, and bound her in her bones." He leaned forward intently. "That was a mistake. We tamed the seas for ourselves, aye, yet opened the door for Beckett and his ilk. Better were the days when mastery of the seas came not through bargains struck with eldritch creatures, but by the sweat of a man's brow and the strength of his back alone. And you all know this be true!"

Despite himself, Jack found himself nodding along with Barbossa's impassioned speech. The nasty man made a rather good argument and the other pirates were nodding as well.

"Gentlemen," Barbossa continued in ringing tones, "ladies . . . we must free Calypso."

Silence fell. Everyone was too shocked to react.

The Indian Pirate Lord beckoned to his bodyguard, Akshay. The large man listened and then stepped forward and spoke.

"Sri Sumbhajee says . . ." Akshay pointed to Barbossa. "He has lost his senses! Do not let him speak any further!"

"Shoot him!" Ammand the Corsair chimed in eagerly.

"Cut out his tongue!" Gentleman Jocard agreed.

"Shoot him and then cut out his tongue!"

Jack cried enthusiastically. "And trim that scraggly beard!" Barbossa glared at him.

Elizabeth spoke up. "Sao Feng would have agreed with Barbossa." She remembered Sao Feng's respect for the sea goddess Calypso, and the way he had looked at her when he thought *she* might be the goddess in human form.

"And I would have agreed with Sao Feng," Villanueva said.

Jocard shook his head vehemently. "Calypso was our enemy then, she will be our enemy now."

"And with far better reason," Chevalle agreed.

Villanueva pulled out his pistol and slammed it on the table. "I would *still* agree with Sao Feng," he growled.

"You threaten me?" Chevalle asked.

"I silence you!" Villanueva shouted. He raised the pistol, but before he could aim, Chevalle punched him in the face, sending the Spaniard sprawling into a group of other pirates. As he fell, the pistol went off, and suddenly the room exploded in chaos. All the pirates began shouting and brawling, pushing and shoving. This was sure to lead to bloodshed and death in no time.

Elizabeth was horrified. "This is madness!" she cried.

"This is politics," said Jack.

Elizabeth could not believe the pirates were fighting at a time like this, when the enemy was so close, and it was so important for them all to stand together. Every time they attacked each other, they were doing Lord Beckett's job for him. If they could not find a way to work together . . . the East India Trading Company was sure to kill them off, one by one.

Deep in the depths of the *Black Pearl*, the subject of the Court's discussion was trapped in the brig. Tia Dalma cast a set of crab claws across the wooden boards, reading their hidden signs. What she saw made her smile. She rose and turned toward a shape emerging from the shadows.

It was Davy Jones.

"You—" Tia Dalma began, but the note of pleasure in her voice vanished when she saw the pistol he was pointing at her. She realized why he was there. "You've come to kill me before the Brethren set me free."

Jones didn't speak; powerful emotion was

overwhelming him. His heart was close enough to affect his feelings, and here in this cabin was the source of the strongest emotions he'd ever felt.

Tia Dalma stepped toward him, her expression tender, but he flinched away as if she'd tried to strike him.

"You fear me?" she said.

"The Brethren's spell stripped you of your memory," Jones said.

"It came back slowly," she said, "over time . . . and with it, some small portion of my power. Enough to rekindle life in Barbossa, when the sea fetched his body up upon my shores." She studied Jones, observing the beard of tentacles, the crab-claw hand, the beady eyes beneath the captain's hat. "Look what you've brought upon yourself," she said sadly. "Many things you were, Davy Jones, but never a monster. Never cruel."

"I learned it from you!" Jones cried, his voice breaking. "Ten years I commanded the *Dutchman*, dispatching the duty you assigned me, but when the time came to step ashore . . . you weren't there!" Anguish twisted his features. "Why weren't you there?" he pleaded.

Tia Dalma shrugged, her fingers playing

across the tentacles of his beard. "It's my nature," she said. "But I may have been there the next time." She leaned coyly toward him. "Would you love me if I was anything but what I am?"

Davy Jones looked away. "I don't love you," he said gruffly.

"That's a shame," Tia Dalma murmured, "because I will be free, and when I am, I would give you my heart." She rested her hand on his empty chest, where he had torn out his own heart to spare himself the pain of her betrayal. Magic spilled out of her into him, and he transformed. His monstrous features melted away, and he stood before her, once again the man he had been— the man she had loved.

"And we would be together, always," Tia Dalma went on, "if only you had a heart to give."

Her hand drifted away from him, and the magic subsided. Davy Jones became a monster again. He stood, shaken, absorbing what she had offered.

Tia Dalma—Calypso—stepped back and spread her hands, leaving herself open to whatever he chose. If he still wanted to shoot her, this was his chance.

Davy Jones slowly returned the pistol to his belt. As he moved back into the shadows, he paused and turned to her.

"The Brethren Court," he asked, "what of them?"

"My captors?" Tia Dalma said, her voice cold with fury. "I have spent centuries not knowing what I was, because of them. . . . Them, all of them . . ." She wrapped a hand around one of the bars of her cell, her knuckles white, her eyes glittering. "They will learn cruelty."

Barbossa banged the cannonball again, trying to restore order. But the noise was too loud for anyone to hear him, and the pirates were too angry to stop fighting. Finally Barbossa hurled the cannonball at the globe, which toppled over, sending swords clattering in all directions. That got their attention at last.

"It was the *first* court that imprisoned Calypso!" Barbossa cried. "*We* can be the ones to set her free! And, in her gratitude, she will show us her favor!"

"Or at least," Jack Sparrow pointed out, "the one of us who summoned the rest of us and convinced all of us to set her free." Barbossa glared at him. "It's not impossible. Is it so improbable?"

"If you have a better alternative, out with it!" Barbossa demanded.

"I agree with Captain Swann," said Jack, astonished to hear those words coming out of his mouth. He stood up, and everyone held their breath waiting to hear what he would say.

"We fight," he said simply.

Barbossa rolled his eyes. "You've always run away from a fight!"

"Calumnious lies!" protested Jack. "I have fought hard and often, in order to run away. We all have, else none of us would be here today, and free." He pointed at Mistress Ching. "We can hole up here for years, but we will have become our own jailers." He turned his accusing finger on Barbossa. "We can release Calypso, but if she's not in a merciful mood, she controls the seas themselves, so there'd be nothing we could run away to. Or on." He raised his fist in the air. "We must embrace the oldest, noblest tradition of piracy. We must fight—to run away."

At last, a plan the pirates could get behind.

Cheers rose from the crews lined against the hull.

Mistress Ching thumped her cane. "And what be the target of this fight, eh?" she demanded.

"Beckett," Elizabeth said instantly.

Chevalle shook his head. "Beckett is naught but a cog. Kill him, another takes his place. Like Jones, the East India Trading Company is immortal. No body to kick or soul to damn."

"Ah," said Jack, "but Jones does have a body, doesn't he? Both literal and figurative."

Jocard realized what he was saying. "And if we kick either hard enough or enough times . . ."

"The *Dutchman* must always have a captain—but if there *is* no *Dutchman* . . ." Ammand finished, "what matters its captain?"

Barbossa sensed that he was losing the room. If he could not convince the Pirate Lords to free Calypso, his whole plan would have failed. And then Tia Dalma would be angry . . . and even with her reduced power, he did not want to make her angry. He had to try a new tack.

"As per the Code," he announced loudly, "an act of war, and this be exactly that, can only be declared by the Pirate King."

"You made that up!" Jack protested.

"Did I now?" Barbossa smiled. "I call on Captain Teague, Keeper of the Code!"

As two pirates darted out of the room, the Indian Lord, Sumbhajee, made a small gesture. His bodyguard Akshay stepped forward. "Sri Sumbhajee proclaims this be folly," he interpreted for his master. "We are not beholden to those ancient, outdated set of laws! Hang the Code! Are we not free to—"

Akshay's speech was abruptly cut off by the sound of a pistol shot. With a surprised expression, Akshay looked down at the blood spreading across his chest. The other pirates watched in alarm as he dropped to the ground, dead.

Behind him stood an old pirate, one many of them had heard of but never seen. He was Captain Teague, Keeper of the Pirate Code. His pistol was still smoking from the fatal shot, and he stared at Sumbhajee ominously.

"The Code is the law," Teague growled.

Sumbhajee beckoned quickly to his other henchman, Pusan, who stepped forward with a nervous look. "Sri Sumbhajee explains that a great misunderstanding has occurred," Pusan said, "and avers that indeed the Code is the law."

The two pirates who had gone to summon Teague re-entered the room, carrying a large, weathered, locked book between them. This was the famous Pirate Code, set down by the first Brethren Court. Pirates all around the room stared in awe.

Teague unlocked the book and opened it. With a thoughtful expression, he thumbed through the pages, keeping one hand on his pistol at all times. Everyone waited expectantly, a tense silence filling the room.

Finally Teague looked up. "Barbossa is right," he said.

Jack stepped over and read the passage himself. Teague scowled, looking as if he was considering shooting Jack.

"'It be the duties of the King to declare war, parlay with foemen, coordinate forces . . .'" Jack read aloud. "Fancy that."

Chevalle snorted. "There's not been a king since the first court, and that's not likely to change."

"Why is that?" Elizabeth whispered to Gibbs.

"See, the king is elected by vote," Gibbs

explained in a low voice, "and each pirate only ever votes for hisself." Elizabeth nodded. That sounded like classic pirate behavior.

"I call for a vote!" shouted Jack.

A murmur of agreement rippled around the room as pirates nodded and whispered to each other.

Ammand the Corsair raised his hand. "I vote for Ammand the Corsair," he declared.

"Capitaine Chevalle," said Chevalle with an elegant gesture, "the penniless Frenchman."

Pusan spoke up for his master. "Sri Sumbhajee declares for Sri Sumbhajee."

The vote continued around the table as expected: Mistress Ching, Gentleman Jocard, Barbossa, and Villanueva all voted for themselves. When it came to Elizabeth, she said "Elizabeth Swann," figuring when with pirates, it was best to do as the other pirates did.

Then the vote came to Jack. With no hesitation, he announced, "I vote in favor of— Elizabeth Swann."

"Me?" Elizabeth said, shocked. "Why?" Shouts of outrage came from the assembled pirates. This was not how the vote was supposed to go! What kind of pirate captain wouldn't vote for himself?

Jack shrugged. He did not particularly care for the throne. After all, the last time he had ended up a ruler was on *Isla de Pelegostos* and that seat had been a little *too* hot. He turned to address the Court. "Am I to understand, then, that we will not keep to the Code?"

"Very well," Mistress Ching said in resignation. "What say you, Captain Swann, King of the Brethren Court?"

The new Pirate King stood and looked around at her new subjects.

"At dawn, we are at war," Elizabeth declared. The decision was made. They would take on the East India Trading Company, destroy the *Dutchman*, and then flee to the safety of the open seas. Barbossa tried to protest, but he was drowned out.

With whoops of glee, the pirates all began to move out to their ships. Elizabeth led the way with a smile—finally they were working together, as she'd wanted.

Glowering, Barbossa signaled to Pintel and Ragetti, who gathered up the scarf with the Pieces of Eight and followed him out.

Last to leave was Jack, who was looking more serious than usual. Looking around the now almost empty room, he noticed Teague watching him.

"What?" Jack said. "You've seen it all. And survived. That's the trick, isn't it? To survive."

Teague shook his head. "It's not just about living forever, Jackie. The trick is, living with yourself forever." He unhooked a shrunken head from his belt and handed it to Jack. Bewildered, Jack accepted it. With a nod, Teague vanished back into the shadows.

Jack paused before turning to leave. His schemes were starting to come together . . . but he still had no idea if they would work out to his benefit. True, he had convinced the Lords to destroy the *Flying Dutchman*, but if the ship were destroyed, so too were his chances for immortality.

This was going to be tricky.

Chapter 19

The *Black Pearl* sailed proudly out of the tunnel, coming up alongside the *Empress*. Jack saluted Elizabeth, one captain to another, and she felt a shiver of apprehension. A real battle lay ahead of them, one that could make a huge difference to the lives of pirates everywhere . . . maybe even save some of them.

Throngs of pirate ships were lined up, all gathered now outside the safety of Shipwreck Island. On every deck, pirates were sharpening swords and readying cannons, preparing for the inevitable action.

An early morning fog lay across the water. At the helm of the *Pearl*, Marty was peering out, searching for shapes in the mist.

Suddenly, a solitary ship appeared through the gray clouds. Marty snapped to attention. It was the *Endeavour*.

"The enemy is here!" Marty yelled at the top of his lungs. "Let's take 'em!"

The other ships responded with bloodcurdling screams of approval as pirates drew their swords and stood forth confidently. One ship against their whole fleet! They would defeat Lord Beckett in no time! Then they'd show him the same mercy he'd shown all those pirates he'd left dying at the end of a hangman's rope.

But then another ship appeared out of the mist. And another. And another. And another.

The cries of the pirates grew less confident, less strong. Their cheers slowly died out as more and more ships came into view. The fog was lifting—and now they could see the full strength of the East India Trading Company's armada. There were hundreds of ships, all manner of sizes, all heavily armed and ready for battle. The fleet of the Pirate Lords looked small beside their vast numbers.

And then the sea began to boil, and a dark ship rose out of the depths to lead Beckett's fleet—the *Flying Dutchman*. The pirates fell silent as its sails broke the surface, and dread plunged into the heart of every pirate as they beheld the gruesome faces of Davy Jones and his men.

Lord Beckett was standing on the deck of the *Endeavour*, pleased to see the reaction from the pirate ships. He lowered his spyglass and smiled. Jack had delivered on his promise to bring the pirates out. "Well played again, Jack," he murmured. "And what's your next move?"

That's what every pirate was wondering. Thousands of angry eyes turned to him, afraid for their lives. He had voted for this battle—now what did he think they should do?

Jack raised his hands in an "oops" gesture. "Parlay?" he suggested.

Not too far from the fleets of gathered ships, there was a sandbar, a sparkling white strip of sand that formed a perfect neutral meeting ground.

Jack, Elizabeth, and Barbossa stepped out of their longboat and walked along the white sand toward the second longboat, from where Lord Beckett, Davy Jones, and Will Turner were approaching. The two threesomes met in the middle and regarded each other.

Barbossa scowled at Will before snarling,

"You be the cur that led these wolves to our door."

"Don't blame Turner," Lord Beckett said archly. "He was but the tool of your betrayal." The aristocrat's eyes slid sideways and he smiled with thin lips. "If you wish to see its grand architect— look to your left."

Elizabeth and Barbossa turned to look at Jack. Acting perplexed, Jack turned and looked to his left as well. Nobody else was there. Jack raised his eyebrows and pressed his hand to his chest.

"Me?" he protested. "My hands are clean in this." He took a look at his hands. "Figuratively," he clarified.

Will agreed. "My actions were my own," he said, "to my own purpose. Jack had nothing to do with it."

"There!" said Jack. "Listen to the tool." Will frowned at him.

"Will," Elizabeth said, and her voice was kinder than the last time he had heard it. He looked into her eyes and saw a new forgiveness, perhaps even sympathy. "I've been aboard the *Dutchman*," she said. "I understand the burden you bear. But I fear that cause is lost." She did not think Bootstrap could be brought back to his true self, and she knew that if Will tried, he would be lost to the *Dutchman* forever.

"No cause is lost if there is but one fool left to fight for it," Will said earnestly. His eyes shifted toward Jack, and Elizabeth noticed. Did they have a plan she didn't know about?

Lord Beckett was not interested in playing games, or in lovers' reunions. He held up Jack's Compass, looking directly at Jack. "If Turner was not acting on your behalf, then how did he come to give me this?"

This evidence was enough to convince Barbossa. Jack must have given Will his Compass so that the East India Trading Company could find Shipwreck Island, the Brethren Court, and the Pirate Lords. Jack was the true traitor amongst them.

"You made a deal with me, Jack," Beckett continued, "to deliver the pirates—and here they are. Don't be bashful; step up and claim your reward." He tossed the Compass to Jack, who caught it, looking guilty.

"And what reward does such chicanery fetch these days?" Barbossa wanted to know.

Beckett pointed at Elizabeth, knowing

what an impact his statement would make. "Her," he said.

Will was shocked. Was it true? Had Jack been playing him as well, with his offer to kill Davy Jones? Was it all an elaborate ruse . . . so that Jack could steal off with Elizabeth?

Beckett went on, relishing the revelation. "When the cannon smoke clears and the Brethren are slaughtered, off he sails on the *Pearl*, Elizabeth in his arms, and the blame dead square upon his rival." He flicked his fingers toward Will.

Everyone considered this. Will was shaken; he wasn't sure what to believe. Jack was so untrustworthy, it was easy to picture him betraying them all that way. But it was also possible that Jack had been misleading Beckett.

Elizabeth was also confused. What would Jack want with her? The *Pearl* she understood, but to take her as well? It did not make sense.

Barbossa, on the other hand, was far from confused. The scheme Beckett had outlined sounded like vintage Jack Sparrow to him.

Jack sighed, as if displeased that Lord Beckett had blown his cover so thoroughly.

"Even *if* that was my plan," he said, "and I'm

not admitting to anything—there's not a tinker's chance of it coming off anymore." He glanced at Elizabeth, then leaned in closer to her. "Is there?" he asked.

She gave him a puzzled look as Beckett said, "There never was."

Davy Jones finally spoke. "Your debt to me must still be satisfied," he said to Jack, his claw snapping. "One hundred years in servitude aboard the *Dutchman* . . . as a start."

Suddenly things clicked into place in Elizabeth's head. The *Dutchman*—Jack's debt—Will's father—the one fool still willing to fight . . . and Jack's determination never to die again. It all made sense. Of course, Jack wouldn't mind killing Davy Jones in exchange for being captain of the *Dutchman*, with immortality in the bargain. And then Will's father would be freed . . . and Will could still be with her.

She looked over at Will, who saw the dawning realization in her eyes. He nodded very slightly. He knew she'd figured out their plan.

Meanwhile, Jack was arguing with Jones.

"That debt was paid," he insisted. He gave a mocking half-bow to Elizabeth. "With some help."

"You escaped," Jones pointed out.

Jack waved his hand airily. "A technicality," he said.

It was time for Elizabeth to speak up, and she knew just what to say. "There's no better end for Jack Sparrow than bilge rat aboard the *Flying Dutchman*," she announced. "I propose an exchange. Will leaves with us . . . and you can have Jack."

"Done," said Will quickly.

"Not done!" Jack objected.

"Done," agreed Beckett.

"Elizabeth, love, you're condemning me," Jack said. "Again."

Elizabeth lifted her hands, palms up.

"Jack is one of the Nine Pirate Lords!" Barbossa protested. He still needed Jack's Piece of Eight to perform the spell to free Calypso. If Jack vanished onto the *Dutchman*—Barbossa might never get the chance to fulfill his bargain with Calypso. "You have no right!" he sputtered.

Elizabeth pointed toward herself. "King," she said simply, reminding him of her new position.

Barbossa frowned. Something more was going on here than met the eye.

"As you command, your nibs," Jack said, doffing his hat. With a heavy sigh, he started forward toward Beckett. Barbossa grabbed his shoulder and pulled him back around, drawing his sword.

"Blaggard!" the old pirate growled.

Jack darted out of reach, but as he moved, his Piece of Eight dropped to the ground. "Jack" the Monkey leaped off Barbossa's shoulder and seized the piece, bringing it back to Barbossa. The two men regarded each other suspiciously.

"If you have something to say," Barbossa snarled, "I might be saying something as well."

"First to the finish, then," Jack said.

He crossed over to the other side of the sandbar, as Will passed on his way to Elizabeth's side. When Jack reached Beckett and Jones, Jones seized his shoulder and shoved him down to the sand.

"Do you fear death?" he snarled.

"You have no idea," answered Jack.

Beckett stepped back, looking pleased with himself. "Advise your 'Brethren': you can fight, and all of you will die," he said. "Or you can not fight, in which case only *most* of you will die."

"You murdered my father," Elizabeth said.

Beckett shrugged. "He chose his own fate."

"And you have chosen yours," Elizabeth said. "We will fight . . . and surely you will die."

"So be it," Beckett said ominously.

Elizabeth and Will turned their backs on their enemies and strode across the sandbar to the longboat.

"King?" Will asked quietly.

"Of the Brethren Court," she explained. "Courtesy of Jack."

Will was impressed. "Maybe he really does know what he's doing." Behind them, "Jack" the Monkey dropped a Piece of Eight into Barbossa's hand, and with a grim look, Barbossa closed his fingers around it.

The parlay was over. It was time for the fight to begin.

189

Chapter 20

Elizabeth was all business as they climbed back on board the *Pearl*. Will and Barbossa followed behind, both scowling, their minds full of Sparrow.

"We'll need the *Black Pearl* to serve as our flagship and lead the attack," she said.

"Will we, now?" Barbossa said. Elizabeth and Will turned to find him holding up Jack's Piece of Eight. Across the deck, they spotted Pintel and some Chinese pirates leading Tia Dalma up on deck. The mystic woman looked tiny under the weight of the manacles, chains, and heavy ropes wrapped around her. But Will and Elizabeth both knew that inside the tiny human figure of Tia Dalma was hidden a powerful sea goddess, full of dark magic that no one on the seas would be able to stand against.

They knew what Barbossa intended to do—release the goddess Calypso from the spell that bound her. Even though the Pirate Lords had not agreed to it, Barbossa had collected their Pieces of Eight after the meeting. That was all he needed. Now he could do it himself, and no one could stop him. There was only one piece missing.

"Barbossa, you can't release her," Will objected.

"Can't I, now?" Barbossa said.

The Pirate Lord signaled, and suddenly Elizabeth and Will were surrounded by Chinese pirates, who quickly restrained them. Meanwhile, Pintel and Ragetti dragged Tia Dalma to the mast and began to bind her in place.

"We've got to give Jack a chance!" Elizabeth protested. If he could break free and kill Davy Jones, then the pirates might have a hope of defeating the East India Trading Company.

"Apologies, Your Highness," Barbossa said, "but 'tis certain the world we know ends today, and I won't be letting the likes of Cutler Beckett say what comes next." He snorted. "And I won't be pinning my hopes on Jack Sparrow, either. Too long has my fate not been in my own hands. No longer!"

Reaching out, he seized the knot pendant

around Elizabeth's neck. Pirates held her back so there was nothing she could do as he added it to the other Pieces of Eight in the scarf-lined bowl that Ragetti held.

As all nine pieces were brought together, the wind suddenly died.

"Is there an incantation?" Elizabeth asked.

"Aye," Barbossa said, holding the bowl. "The items brought together, done. Has to be performed over water; we lucked out there. Items burned. And some person must speak the words, 'Calypso, I release you from your human bonds.'"

"Is that it?" Pintel asked.

"Twas said it must be spoken softly, as if to a lover," Barbossa said. He grabbed a rum bottle and smashed it over the pile of objects. With a firebrand, he lit the pile, now doused in rum. Smoke rose instantly from the bowl, with orange flames flickering in its depths.

"Calypso," Barbossa called loudly, "I release you from your human bonds!"

Everyone turned to stare at Tia Dalma. Nothing happened.

"You didn't say it right!" Ragetti protested. As the stares turned toward him, he bristled defensively. "You have to say it right."

Ragetti stepped up to Tia Dalma, his voice full of sincere love for the sea. "Calypso," he murmured, "I release you from your human bonds."

The bowl burst into flames. The fire shot up in a twisting column, and then just as suddenly it vanished, and all that was left of the Pieces of Eight were bits of ashes and metal.

Tia Dalma gasped, doubling over. Rust crept across the manacles around her wrists, pitting them with corrosion. She shuddered violently, and they broke apart, falling to the deck in a shower of orange metal dust.

The eyes of the sea goddess glowed with long-suppressed power. She stretched out her hands as the magic returned to her.

"Tia Dalma! Calypso!" Will cried. She turned her smoldering eyes to him, her expression still confused, as if she were waking from a long sleep. Will spoke urgently. There was only one chance to turn her in the right direction. "When the Brethren Court first imprisoned you," he said, "who was it that told them how? Who was it that betrayed you?"

"Name him," said Calypso in a voice that rang with authority and old magic.

"Davy Jones," Will said.

She whirled to stare at the *Dutchman*, hate and rage building in her eyes. With a howl of fury, Tia Dalma began to grow, transforming right before them into a towering creature that barely seemed human anymore. Her hair rippled even though there was no wind; the deck buckled under her weight as she rose up taller and taller and taller.

Barbossa knelt in front of her. "Calypso," he called. "I come before you as a servant, humble and contrite. I have fulfilled my vow, and now ask your favor. Spare my self, my ship, my crew—but unleash your fury upon those who dare pretend themselves your masters, or mine!"

The sea goddess barely glanced at him. Her voice boomed across the deck, resonating through the fleet. "FOOL!" she howled.

Barbossa's eyes went wide. Had his gamble failed? The risk had been great for a great reward—but would it all have been for nothing?

And then, all at once, the goddess collapsed, crashing down to the deck in a shower of ten thousand crabs. A torrent of crabs swarmed across the ship, scattering pirates in all directions, flooding toward the edge. In an instant, the crabs flowed over the sides of the ship into the water, and Calypso was gone. The goddess of the sea had vanished completely.

The pirates, struck speechless, gawked for a moment.

Finally, Will said, "Is *that* it?"

"Why, she's no help at all!" said Pintel. "What now?" he asked Barbossa.

The wind stirred again, and the sails began to fill.

"Nothing," said Barbossa. "Our final hope has failed us."

The pirates fell silent again, this time out of despair. If Barbossa had given up . . . was there any hope for any of them?

The wind grew stronger, and a pirate's hat was lifted off his head. As it spiraled up and around the mast, Elizabeth watched it, feeling something else stirring inside her.

"It's not over," she said.

Will turned to her, his heart lifting at the sound of the courage in her voice. "Hope is not lost," he agreed. "There's still a fight to be had."

"There's an armada arrayed against us," Gibbs pointed out. "We've got no chance of winnin'."

Elizabeth looked up at the hat again. The wind was blowing even stronger now, and the hat was whipped about in the air. "Only a fool's chance . . ." she murmured.

"Revenge won't bring your father back, Miss Swann," Barbossa said. Elizabeth reacted as if she'd been slapped. Was that her true motive? She searched inside herself.

Barbossa kept speaking. "And it's not something I'm intending to die for," he said sharply.

It was true. Nothing could bring her father back, and Elizabeth knew it.

"You're right," she said. She looked around at the pirates, all believing in her as their King. There was more to this than revenge—much more. "Then what shall we all die for?" she asked.

If Jack could free himself . . . and find his way to the chest . . . and stab the heart of Davy Jones. . . . It was a long shot, but if anyone could do it, it was Captain Jack Sparrow. And he'd be counting on them to fight as well. He couldn't do this alone. No pirate could survive on his own for long. That was why they had ships and crews; no matter how much they fought, there was still the Pirate Code, and a pirate's life was lived as part of a team . . . part of a crew. They had to work together, or they would each die alone.

She leaped up onto the rail of the ship, looking out at the crewmen around her. Their eyes turned to her, and she could see how much they wanted to believe.

"Listen to me," she called. "The Brethren will still be looking here, to us, to the *Black Pearl*, to lead. What will they see?" Elizabeth cried. "Frightened bilge rats aboard a derelict ship? No. They will see free men. And freedom!" She raised her fist in the air. "And what the enemy will see is the flash of our cannons. They will hear the ring of our swords. And they will know what we can do, by the sweat of our brows and the strength of our backs—and the courage of our hearts."

She met each pirate's eyes, as they looked up to her with dawning hope on their faces. Finally, she turned to Will.

"Hoist the colors," she said.

Elizabeth drew her sword and pointed it toward the *Endeavour*.

Chapter 21

The call to arms had been raised by the Pirate King. Now, all around the *Black Pearl*, pirates aboard other ships let out mighty cheers and prepared to fight the East India Trading Company. Jolly Rogers were raised and began to whip in the gathering wind. On board each ship, captains shouted orders and pirates leaped into action.

"Target the *Flying Dutchman*," Will shouted aboard the *Pearl*. "We're the only ship that can catch her."

While the pirates rushed about their ships, pistols drawn and revenge on their faces, Beckett stood quietly on the deck of the *Endeavor*, sipping tea. His face showed no signs of worry and his pristine white wig was perfectly set upon his head. Looking out at the ragtag fleet of pirate ships, he repressed a satisfied smile. He was not worried. Calypso had been released to no consequence. Further, Beckett was still in control of the *Dutchman*. Looking up, he took in the increasing wind. Turning to one of his officers, he nodded. It was time. "Signal Jones," he ordered.

From his spot on the upper deck of the *Dutchman*, Mercer spotted the signal flag raised by the *Endeavour*. "To arms!" he cried out. All around him, the ship's barnacled crew let out a roar of approval. This was the moment they had been waiting for.

But not everyone on the *Dutchman* was as excited. Davy Jones noticed the increasing wind and, slowly, his tentacled hand reached for the spot where his heart used to be. "Calypso . . ." he said softly. Only he recognized the power of the goddess. And she had not yet even begun to show her true strength.

The sky continued to grow darker and gray clouds began to quickly churn. They formed a circle high in the sky, directly above the ships— pirate and Company, alike. Lightning split the sky, illuminating the eerie scene and revealing something far more dangerous than the storm clouds.

In the middle of the turquoise Caribbean waters, a large whirlpool was slowly beginning to turn. Rain began to fall in sheets, soaking everyone and making it harder to tell one ship from another. On board the *Black Pearl*, Gibbs stared out at the sea. In all his years aboard seafaring vessels, he had never seen anything like this. "Maelstrom!" he shouted, finding his voice. "Saints preserve us!"

As the storm's fury increased, Elizabeth looked around at the shocked crew. All of them seemed to have been shaken by Gibbs's announcement. But now was not the time for fear.

"Captain Barbossa!" Elizabeth shouted. "I need you at the helm."

Looking over at Elizabeth, Barbossa nodded. "Aye, that be true! Brace up yards, you cack-handed deck apes! Dying is the day worth living for!"

Slowly, the *Black Pearl* was steered away from the maelstrom. And all around her, every other ship turned away as well—the battle against each other forgotten in an attempt to save themselves. But as the others successfully sailed out of the reach of the giant whirlpool, the *Pearl* struggled.

The *Flying Dutchman*, too, was struggling against the maelstrom. At her helm, Mercer was spinning the wheel, hoping to keep the ship far from the edges of the whirlpool. But it was proving too difficult. Walking over to the wheel, Jones's cold eyes looked down at Mercer. "Shall not harm us!" he shouted through the pouring rain. "Full-bore, and into the abyss!"

"Are you mad?" Mercer screamed.

"Are you afraid to get wet?" Jones sneered. Then, turning to the crew—his crew—he ordered, "Stand on!" In one swift movement, he wrestled the wheel from Mercer and gave it a mighty spin. The *Dutchman* slipped over the edge . . . straight into the maelstrom.

Meanwhile the *Black Pearl* had also slipped inside the rim of the whirling water and was now being carried along at the topmost part of maelstrom. Within moments, the *Dutchman* had found a spot deeper in the whirlpool, where the water was moving at a swifter speed. She quickly moved in behind the *Pearl's* stern.

Will turned in time to see the *Dutchman* slip into a position that gave her the clear advantage. "She's on our stern and gaining!" he shouted.

"More speed!" Barbossa ordered in response, all too aware of what was happening. With no way to move out of the other ship's way, the *Pearl* was defenseless.

Suddenly, the sound of cannon fire split the air. Moments later, cannonballs hit the *Pearl's* stern and crashed onto the deck, splitting wood and hitting one of the helm's steering pins. "Take us out!" Will shouted. "Before they overbear us!"

"Nay, further in!" answered Barbossa. "Cut across to faster waters!"

Despite the driving rain and the unnatural tilt of the ship, Elizabeth and Will raced down the deck, shouting orders and preparing the crew. They were going to come around and face the *Dutchman* head on!

As the Pearl slipped into her new position, Will looked out at the *Dutchman*. For a moment, he did not move. On that ship was his father *and* Jack Sparrow.

Will's thoughts were interrupted as the two ships moved across from each other. Around them, the rest of the ships disappeared in the heavy mist that had been created by the maelstrom. Belowdecks on the *Pearl*, Pintel and Ragetti prepared the cannons, while across the way, two of Jones's crew did the same.

"Fire!" ordered Barbossa.

"Fire!" ordered Davy Jones.

And amid the pouring rain, crashing lightning, and rushing water, two of the greatest ships to ever sail the Seven Seas started to battle.

Chapter 22

Inside the brig of the *Flying Dutchman,* Jack Sparrow was trying desperately to free himself. Unfortunately, he was once again plagued by the other Jacks from Davy Jones's Locker. They were sitting on his shoulders, giving him advice that he was in no mood to hear.

"Think like the whelp, think like his whelp," the real Jack chanted as he attempted to use a bench to open the prison door.

"Half-barrel hinges!" the tiny Jack on his right shoulder exclaimed. "Leverage"

"Never work," Jack on the left scoffed.

With a grunt, Jack shoved down on the bench one more time, and with a creak and groan, the door fell open. "Wish us luck, boys," he said to his tiny friends, who had moved off his shoulders and were now standing inside the cell. "We might need it." Daintily stepping through the door, he nodded a good-bye and moved toward the deck.

As he walked away, one of the tiny Jacks sighed. "I miss him already."

"He'll be back," the other one said.

Up on deck, cannonballs crashed into the *Dutchman*. But Davy Jones paid them no mind. His attention was focused on Mercer, who stood beside two Company guards, shouting orders at the crew.

Suddenly, another cannon blast sounded through the air. In one quick movement, Jones pushed Mercer out of the way, while the cannon fire took out the two guards behind them. Looking up in relief, Mercer's expression quickly turned to horror as he saw Jones's expression. Before he could move, Jones's beard reached out and wrapped around Mercer's neck, strangling him. A moment later, Mercer collapsed. As he fell, Jones's tentacle held on to the one thing that could return his freedom—the key that would unlock his chest. With a smile, he moved away from Mercer's lifeless body.

Meanwhile, inside the captain's cabin,

Murtogg and Mullroy stood behind two large cannons as they watched over the Dead Man's Chest. Both looked a bit worse for the wear, twitching and jumping at the thundering sounds of the battle. Then the cabin door swung open, and Jack Sparrow waltzed in, looking rather unperturbed by the goings-on.

"Halt there, or we'll shoot!" Mullroy shouted.

Jack stopped and took in the two guards, the huge cannons, and the chest. Jack had dealt with these two before. Reaching up, he twirled one of the braids on his chin between his long fingers. "I just came to see my effects," he said. Then, he added, "Admirable though it is, why are you here when you could be somewhere else?"

"Someone has to stay and guard the chest," Murtogg answered, standing bolt upright.

"No question, there's been a breakdown in military discipline aboard this vessel," Mullroy added.

Murtogg nodded thoughtfully. "I blame the fish people."

"Oh, so the fish people, by dint of being fish people, automatically aren't as disciplined as non-fish people?" Mullroy asked angrily.

As the two marines continued to argue, Jack began to move closer and closer to the chest.

"If there were no chest, there would be nothing to guard," Murtogg said, turning to look at said chest.

Both men gasped. The chest was gone! And so was Jack Sparrow.

Jack was moving as quickly as possible *away* from the captain's cabin. Which proved extremely difficult given the odd tilt of the ship and the chest in his arms. Reaching the stairs, he looked up—just in time to see Davy Jones walking down, flanked by his corrosive crew.

"Lookee boys!" Jones said, catching sight of Jack. "A lost bird that never learned to fly!"

The crewmen laughed as they surged forward, coming a bit too close for Jack's liking. "To my great regret," Jack replied. Looking around, his eyes landed on a sail that lay partially free directly below an opening to the deck. Turning back to Jones, he added, "But it's never too late, eh?" Then, before Jones or his crew could do a thing, Jack released the sail. In a moment, it filled with wind and carried Jack, and the chest, up to the safety of the rigging.

Landing on the yardarm, Jack straightened up and smiled, quite pleased with himself. Inching forward, he moved toward the mast as around him the wind whipped and rain fell.

Suddenly a shadow fell across him and Jack looked up. Davy Jones stood in front of him, sword drawn and murder in his eyes. "The chest," he snarled. "Hand it over."

Jack drew his own sword. "I can set you free, Jones."

"Have you never loved, Jack? My freedom was forfeit long ago." Then, with a roar, Jones leapt at Jack, their swords clashing.

Chapter 23

As Jack and Jones dueled high in the rigging of the *Dutchman*, the maelstrom continued to draw the two ships closer and closer together. Their masts tilted precariously, now almost touching. Crew members began to leap back and forth between the ships while cannons continued to blaze and swords continued to clash.

On board the *Black Pearl*, Will and Elizabeth found themselves fighting off the crew of the *Dutchman*. Working together, they cut and parried. As Will watched his beloved fight bravely, his heart ached. This woman was everything he could ever want. He could not lose her. Not again.

Then, for a moment, there was a break in the fighting. Turning to Elizabeth, Will looked at her intently. "Will you marry me?" he asked.

Elizabeth stopped short, her mind whirling.

Had she heard correctly? Was Will actually asking her to marry him—*now*? As her thoughts raced, another group of attackers moved in. "Right now is not the best time!" she shouted as her sword slashed through the air. Moving around the capstan in opposite directions, they continued to fight off their attackers and for a moment there was no noise but the clashing of steel.

Then, they met again and, with a laugh, Will answered, "Right now may be the only time! I love you!"

For another moment, they were pulled apart. But Will was not going to give up so easily. Reaching out, he grabbed her hand. "I've made my choice," he said boldly. "What's yours?"

Elizabeth looked deep in his eyes and had no question. This was the man she loved. She would not let him go. With a glint in her eye, she shouted, "Barbossa!" Will looked down at his beloved in confusion. But a moment later, it all became clear. "Marry us!" she shouted.

On the deck above them, Barbossa was busy fighting off several of the *Dutchman's* crew. "I'm a little busy at the moment," he answered.

But Will was not going to take no for an

answer. As he and Elizabeth continued to fight, he called out, "Barbossa! Now!"

Barbossa groaned. Pushing aside a few more attackers, he made his way over to a raised platform near the helm. Looking down, he watched as Elizabeth and Will made their way closer together, while their swords continued to swing. "Dearly beloved and others, we are gathered here—" He was interrupted as another attacker came close.

Below, Elizabeth and Will also were attacked by yet more hideous, cursed crewman. Not exactly the wedding party they had imagined. As they fought down the length of the deck, Will continued the ceremony, "Elizabeth Swann, do you take me to be your husband?"

"I do," she answered. "Will Turner, do you take me to be your wife?"

"I do," Will answered, smiling even as he swung his sword.

Back by the wheel, Barbossa had managed to get clear of his attackers. Now he wanted his big moment. Looking out over the deck, he shouted, "As Captain, I pronounce you . . ." Another barnacled pirate attacked, but Barbossa pushed him away. "You may kiss—kiss the—the kiss!"

On the deck, Will did not wait for Barbossa to finish. He reached out and for a moment, their lips almost met. But then they were pulled apart.

Will suppressed a groan of rage. He would kiss Elizabeth! They would make this official. Struggling through the attackers, he pushed and kicked his way toward her. Then, as all around them, the fight continued, he leaned down and kissed her. It was a kiss full of passion, full of the promises to come, and, full of apologies for things that could never be undone.

Chapter 24

High up on the yardarm, as the storm raged on, Jack Sparrow and Davy Jones continued to spar. Back and forth they parried across the narrow planks. Finally, with a powerful jab, Jack knocked Jones's sword out his tentacled hand.

"There is nothing you can do with that," Jones sneered, nodding at the chest that Jack still clung to, "without the key."

"I already have the key," Jack answered with a sly smile.

Hearing those words, Jones paused and for a moment, his eyes filled with fear. Was it possible? Then, the fear left, and Jones smiled. One of the tentacles on his beard twisted and writhed before revealing the very key. "No, you don't," Jones stated.

As Jones spoke, the tentacle moved out and displayed the key dangling at the end. Jack looked intently at it, his khol-lined eyes revealing nothing. "Oh, *that* key," he said, as though surprised. Then, in one swift move, Jack reached out with his sword and sliced through the tentacle. As black ink spurted everywhere, the key dropped down through the rigging, landing with a clink on the deck, still clutched in the writhing tentacle.

With a roar of rage, Jones lunged at Jack, shoving him back. As the ship whirled and the rain fell, the two men fought across the yardarm—Jack at a distinct disadvantage as he still clutched the chest in his hand. Suddenly, the masts of the two ships collided across the narrowing abyss, causing the timber to shake.

Up on the yardarm, the force of the collision caused Jack to lose his balance and as both men watched, the Dead Man's Chest slipped slowly out of Jack's hands.

"No!" roared Jones. In one swift move, he leaned out and grabbed the chest with his tentacled hand. But it was oddly heavy. Looking down, Jones spotted Jack, dangling on to the other end.

For a moment, neither Jones nor Jack did a thing. Then, with a mighty heave, Jones began to swing the chest through the air—and Jack with it! Jack had no choice. Letting go of the chest, he reached out to grab a line, freeing himself of Jones. As he dangled high above the deck, he noticed one of Jones's crew members swing by carrying his pistol! Jack reached out and grabbed the pistol. Then, he aimed and fired, hitting Jones and sending the chest crashing to the deck below.

Meanwhile back aboard the *Pearl*, Will Turner had taken notice of the fight high in the rigging. He knew that his only hope in freeing his father was Jack's success. If the rascally captain did not stab Jones's heart and take his place, Bootstrap would never be free. He had to do something—fast. Grabbing a line, he strode over to the *Pearl's* rail and, without a backward glance, swung over to the *Dutchman*.

While the scene aboard the *Pearl* had been chaotic, the *Dutchman* was even more so. Barnacled, sea-covered crew members raced this way and that, slashing and cutting at anything that crossed their path. And in the middle of it all was the Dead Man's Chest. Will quickly picked up the chest and began to back away, hoping to make it to the *Pearl* before he was spotted. But luck was not on his side.

Davy Jones had made his way out of the rigging and was now striding across the deck, a murderous gleam in his eye. Turning to look behind him, Will noticed that Maccus, Jones's first mate, was blocking his path. He was trapped! There was nowhere to . . .

Suddenly, another cannon explosion rocked the air, and a moment later, "Jack" the Monkey slammed into Maccus, knocking him out of the way. Taking advantage of the distraction, Will continued to move across the deck. But then, he, too, found himself knocked to the ground. The chest slipped from his grip as he shook his head in confusion.

Looking up, he found himself staring at his father—or rather, what was left of his father. Bootstrap began to slash at Will with his sword.

"Stop!" cried Will, as he parried his sword to ward off the blows. This was not the reunion he had hoped for.

Chapter 25

While Will and his father continued to fight on board the *Dutchman*, the crew of the *Pearl* was desperately trying to break free of the maelstrom's hold.

At the *Pearl's* wheel, Barbossa strained to keep the two ships apart as the swirling waters dragged them closer and closer together.

"She's taking us down!" Barbossa yelled out, as his hands gripped the wheel. "Make quick, or it's the Locker for us all!"

From where she stood, Elizabeth heard Barbossa's desperate shout. But her mind was not on the ships or getting free. Her mind was on Will. Glancing over at Gibbs, she gave the old pirate a knowing look.

"I've got it—go!" Gibbs shouted.

That was all Elizabeth needed to hear. Turning, she raced for the *Dutchman*—and her husband.

Meanwhile, on that very ship, Davy Jones and Jack Sparrow were still engaged in a duel, each desperate to get his hands on the unattended chest. Jones slashed at Jack, causing the pirate to fall backward, just in time to see Elizabeth swing onto the deck. She landed with a thud—right in front of the chest.

"You'll see no mercy from me!" Jones shouted, advancing toward Elizabeth.

But Elizabeth was prepared. "That's why I brought this," she said, raising her sword.

Sneering, Jones lunged and the two began to fight—Jack, and the chest, momentarily forgotten.

Meanwhile, Will and his father were also still locked in battle. Seeing an opening, Will lunged at his father, disarming him and slamming him against the rail. Pulling out his knife, he raised it high. His hand quivered as he looked down at his father. "I will not kill you," he said. "I made you a promise." Then, he slammed the knife down through Bootstrap's jacket, pinning him to the rail. Without another word, he rushed to assist Elizabeth.

And Elizabeth was in desperate need of

help. Jones was proving to be quite the adversary. Elizabeth's and Jones's swords clashed again and again as they fought their way around the chest.

Under cover of the fight, Jack Sparrow rolled out of the way, only to find himself looking straight at the key to Jones's chest! Darting out his hand, Jack wrestled the key free from the tentacle that still clutched it. Then he smiled. Fortune had turned in his favor.

Unfortunately, the same could not be said for Elizabeth, as Jones smashed her across the face with his clawed hand. For a moment, there was a look of pure satisfaction on his face. But it was quickly replaced by confusion. Looking down, he saw a sword sticking out of his chest. Looking over his shoulder, he saw Will Turner, who was still grasping the sword's hilt.

"Did you forget? I am a heartless wretch!" Reaching down, he bent the sword tip with his bare tentacled hand. As Will stood there, stunned, Jones wrenched sideways, slamming Will to the ground. Looking down at the young man, Jones noticed Will's eyes dart desperately toward Elizabeth. He also noticed Elizabeth's expression.

"Ah. Love," Jones sneered, as he moved closer to Will. "A dreadful bond."

Will pushed himself back quickly, looking for an escape but not finding one.

"Yet so easily severed," Jones continued. As he talked, he pulled the sword out of his chest and cast it aside. Then he raised his own sword. "Tell me, William Turner. Do you fear death?"

As the rain poured down, Jones held his sword high. Fear filled Will's eyes.

Suddenly, Jones cried out in anguish.

"Do *you*?" Jack asked.

All eyes turned to see the one and only Captain Jack Sparrow, standing above the open Dead Man's Chest, Jones's still-beating heart in his hand. With a smile on his lips and a glint in his khol-lined eyes, he squeezed the heart. Jones groaned and clutched at his chest. "It's a heady tonic," Jack continued. "Holding life and death in the palm of your hand."

"You are a cruel man, Jack Sparrow," Jones hissed. "Self-serving and dishonest."

Jack paused, as if thinking over Jones's words. Then he shrugged. "Self-serving and dishonest I'll give you, but cruel is a matter of perspective, is it not?"

"Is it?" Jones asked. Then, he turned and stabbed Will—straight through the heart.

Screaming, Elizabeth raced to Will, kneeling down and placing his head in her lap.

Jack looked from the heart to his sword, and back again. Then he looked at Will, lying in the arms of Elizabeth.

"Take what you want most, Jack," Jones said, looking knowingly at the pirate. "Live forever. . . ."

Before Jones could finish his sentence, however, Bootstrap rammed into him, sending Jones flying into the side of the ship. The cursed pirate had seen everything, and whatever human part of him was left could not sit idly by and watch his son die. Pulling himself free, he had attacked. Now he would do whatever it took to save his son.

Chapter 26

As the rain continued to pour down, the maelstrom grew in strength, sucking the *Flying Dutchman* and the *Black Pearl* deeper and deeper into the sea. At the helm of the *Pearl*, Barbossa struggled to keep the ship from falling into the abyss, while back on the *Dutchman*, Jack struggled to figure out what to do. He looked down at Will, then at Elizabeth, then at the heart, then back to Will, and finally back to Elizabeth. Rain streamed down her face, combining with her tears. Looking up at him, she uttered one single word, "Please."

Over at the rail, Jones and Bootstrap were locked in combat, each determined to rid the ship of the other. With one mighty shove, Jones forced Bootstrap out over the rail. One more push, and Bootstrap would be sent to the depths—again. "You will not forestall *my* judgement," Jones snarled. Suddenly, Jones's claw reached toward his chest and he cried out in pain and torment.

Looking over, the last thing Jones saw before he fell over the rail and into the depths of his own locker, was his heart, finally still, stabbed by Jack's sword. Holding the hilt, was Will.

Davy Jones was no more.

Meanwhile, the two ships had become entangled, and back on the *Pearl*, every crew member was trying to free their ship's mast from the mast of the *Dutchman*. Pintel and Ragetti prepared a cannon, lighting the fuse and sending a shot straight across the abyss and into the *Dutchman's* mast. Barbossa, meanwhile, frantically turned the wheel, steering the *Pearl* away from the swirling vortex. Suddenly, the two ships separated, the *Pearl* moved away from the abyss, and the *Dutchman* moved deeper into it.

On the *Dutchman's* deck, Will lay motionless in Elizabeth's arms. Tears streamed down her face as she looked into his warm brown eyes. There was so much she wanted to say. So many things she had never told him. For a moment, Will struggled to speak, but the effort was too great. With a sigh, he slumped in Elizabeth's arms, the life fading from his body.

"Will," Elizabeth cried, her voice cracking. But it was too late.

Slowly, Jones's old crew began to circle around Will's lifeless body. From his spot on the rail, Bootstrap pulled a knife out of the wood and moved closer. Knowing what would happen next, Jack grabbed Elizabeth and pulled her away. She struggled for an instant and then slumped in his arms, the grief overcoming her.

As Jack pulled her away, the crew drew tighter around Will's body. One of them held the Dead Man's Chest in his arms, the lid open, the chest empty. They began to speak in hushed tones, their voices carrying in the wind.

"The *Dutchman* must have a captain," Bootstrap said.

"The *Dutchman* must have a living heart," Maccus added.

Then, altogether, the rest of the crew began to murmur, "Part of the ship, part of the crew, part of the ship, part of the crew . . ."

As the crew chanted, Bootstrap kneeled

down in front of his son and pulled open his shirt. He raised his knife . . .

Before Elizabeth could see what was about to occur on the *Dutchman's* deck, Jack reached over and grabbed one of the lines attached to a flapping sail. Aiming his pistol, he fired, freeing the sail, which quickly filled with air and lifted them off the deck, toward the freedom of the Caribbean sky. Below them, the *Dutchman* slipped deeper and deeper into the whirlpool and then, disappeared into the inky black abyss.

A moment later, the maelstrom calmed and the seas turned flat. The storm was over. . . .

Chapter 27

Jack and Elizabeth landed with a splash in the ocean. Nearby, the *Pearl* floated, a bit worse for the wear, but in one piece. Gibbs, noticing his captain and Elizabeth splashing about, quickly pulled them out.

"Thank heaven Jack," he exclaimed as he hauled the dripping captain onto the *Pearl's* deck. "The armada is still out there, the *Endeavour* is coming up hard starboard, and I think it's time we embraced the oldest, noblest of pirate traditions."

Wringing out his bandolier and cocking his head, Jack answered, "I've never been one for tradition." Then, moving toward the wheel, he began to bark orders.

On board the *Endeavour*, Lord Cutler Beckett stood at the helm, his eyes trained on the *Pearl*. While he was far from pleased with the outcome of the maelstrom, he was still confident that he could best the wily pirates—including Sparrow. As he watched, the *Pearl* continued to sit still in the water, her sails luffing in the wind.

"What's he waiting for?" asked Groves, one of Beckett's lieutenants.

"He expects us to honor our agreement," replied Beckett. Then he shrugged.

Back on the *Pearl*, Jack and Gibbs stood at the rail looking at Beckett's ship which was fast approaching.

"I never figured it was to end like this," Gibbs said with a sigh. "Always pictured an angry husband."

Jack nodded. "Reasonable."

Just as the *Endeavour* drew close enough to fire, the water began to churn and boil. And then, from the depths of the sea, the *Flying Dutchman* emerged. Gone were the encrusted hull and dark sails. Instead, her sides gleamed, and her sails were a brilliant white. Her crew was no longer encrusted with sea-life or flotsom and jetsam— they were the men they had once been. And the ship was once again what she was always meant to be—pure and clean. Then, onto the deck strode her captain—Will Turner—fully alive, revenge in his eyes.

Taking in this sudden development, Jack Sparrow smiled. He might make it out of this predicament alive, after all. Turning, he shouted to his men. "Full canvas!" Within moments, the two ships had sailed up on either side of the *Endeavour*, trapping her—and Beckett.

From where he stood, Beckett stared out across at Jack. It was over—Beckett had failed to destroy the pirates and now, it appeared, they would destroy him.

As marines jumped overboard and leapt into longboats, Beckett remained motionless, as if paralyzed by the sight of both mighty ships. Then, Will's voice rang out loud and clear. "Fire!" he ordered.

"Fire!" shouted Barbossa and Elizabeth.

"Fire," said Jack, a little more quietly than the others.

Cannons blasted again and again as the *Endeavour* was rocked with explosions. When the smoke and debris cleared, the pirates that had remained through the maelstrom, let out a mighty shout. The *Endeavour* had been destroyed. With a creak, her mast fell, crashing through the deck. Ever so slowly, the ship—with Beckett still aboard—began to sink beneath the cool, blue Caribbean sea.

Meanwhile, all around the sinking *Endeavour*, the rest of Beckett's armada began to flee.

"They're running!" shouted Marty.

"Aye," Gibbs replied. "They're terrified to take on the combined might of the *Dutchman* and the *Pearl*."

Jack Sparrow watched the armada of ships. A smile tugged at his mouth. "I've never seen a retreat from the other side before," he said slowly. "Gibbs, you may fling my hat."

Grabbing the captain's beloved tricorn, Gibbs threw it high in the air, celebrating the pirates long-awaited victory.

On board the *Dutchman*, the mood was not as festive. Standing on the deck, Captain William Turner looked out at the *Black Pearl*, his eyes sad. After everything he and Elizabeth had gone through, it appeared that they truly were destined to never be together.

"Orders, sir," came a voice from behind Will. It was Bootstrap.

"You're no longer bound to the *Dutchman*," Will said, surprised by his father's presence. "You're free."

"By my reckoning, I've still got a debt that needs be paid," he paused, before adding, "if you'll have me."

Will was overcome with emotion as he stared hard at his father. Then, fighting back the urge to hug Bootstrap, Will gestured toward the wheel. "On the wheel then, Mr. Turner."

Turning back to the *Pearl*, Will's gaze once again sought out Elizabeth. Bootstrap noticed, and his heart ached for his son. "One day at shore, ten years at sea. It's a steep price to pay for what's been done," he said softly.

For the first time since he stepping on deck, Will smiled. "That depends on the one day."

A short while later, aboard the *Black Pearl*, the crew gathered to send Elizabeth off. She was to make for land . . . and Will. Holding out his hand, Gibbs, gestured to a waiting longboat. "Your chariot awaits. Oars are inside."

Her eyes gleaming, Elizabeth took a step closer, walking past Barbossa. "Mrs. Turner," he said, tipping his feathered hat.

She nodded and continued on her way. When she arrived at the longboat, Jack Sparrow stood beside it, his eyes unreadable.

Elizabeth stopped and smiled, a bit sadly. "Jack Sparrow," she said. "It never would have worked out between us."

"You keep telling yourself that." Then, unable to help himself, he made one last attempt at Elizabeth's heart. "Every king needs a queen," he said softly, leaning close, their lips almost brushing. Then, he pulled away. Elizabeth's heart would always belong to another. And his would always belong to the *Pearl*.

With one last smile, Elizabeth turned and boarded the longboat. It was time to go to Will.

The sun was lowering on the horizon as Will sat on a rock, looking out at the ocean. It was the last time he would be allowed to step foot on land for ten more years. He wanted the moment to last forever.

Coming up behind him, Elizabeth wrapped her arms around Will, a smile on her face as she, too, took in the horizon. But with Will's next words, her smile vanished.

"Nearly sunset," he pointed out, as Elizabeth unwrapped her arms and sat down beside him. "Whatever fate awaits me . . . I don't expect the world to stop turning."

Elizabeth looking at him, realization dawning. He was beginning to say his good-byes. Soon, he would be back on the *Flying Dutchman*, taking up Jones's charge of ferrying dead souls. She would be left alone.

Trying to ignore her stricken expression, Will went on. "We both have obligations already . . . and I am asking you to take on another." Turning, he pulled his coat off of the sand, revealing the Dead Man's Chest. "Will you keep this safe?"

"Yes," Elizabeth answered immediately, taking the chest and cradling it in her arms. This was the one way she could stay close to Will no matter where the sea took him. She would guard it with her life.

"I love you, Elizabeth," Will said simply. Finally free to say what he had felt for so many years. "Always."

"And I you," she answered.

Smiling, his eyes full of regret and love, Will stooped, picked up his coat and walked to the water's edge. Before his toes could touch the waves, Elizabeth's voice rang out, "Will!" she shouted, rushing over and flinging her arms around him in one last embrace.

"You will come back to me," she said.

"Keep a weather eye," Will answered.

Elizabeth's eyes closed as Will leaned down for one final kiss. When she opened them, he was gone, while out on the sea, the *Dutchman's* sails unfurled.

Elizabeth had no idea what the future held for her or Will. Nor did she know what would become of the Brethren Court, Barbossa, and most important, Captain Jack Sparrow. What she did know, was, for this one moment, the world was as it should be—with pirates free to sail the seas, and countless souls in the safe hands of the new captain of the *Flying Dutchman*, Will Turner.

Chapter 28

Captain Jack Sparrow found himself in familiar company. After narrowly escaping the maelstrom and *almost* capturing immortality, he had made his way back to the one port he could count on— Tortuga. Now, with two women—the redheaded Scarlett and the blond Giselle—on his arms, he made his way down the dock.

"Granted, it tends to list to port," Jack said, "but I promise you will not be disappointed."

"Is that it? The *Black Pearl*," Giselle said when they arrived at a rather small, and unimpressive vessel.

"Please, love," Jack scoffed. "That is a dingy. My vessel is magnificent and fierce and . . . gone? Why is it gone?" Looking out to where the *Pearl* was *supposed* to be, Jack saw nothing but empty water.

Suddenly, Giselle pointed further out to sea. "Is that it there?" she asked.

"Yes, there. There it is. Why is it there?" Jack said flatly. The *Pearl* was *not* where he had docked it. In fact, it was sailing away *without him.*

"But Jack, you promised me a ride," Giselle said, her brightly painted lips forming a pout.

Scarlett raised an eyebrow. "What. You?"

As the two women began to bicker, Jack fumed. It had happened again! How was a pirate supposed to make an honest living if every time he turned his back, someone was taking his ship? Spotting Gibbs dozing in a shaded spot on the dock, Jack made his way over.

"Mr. Gibbs," Jack said, a gold tooth gleaming in the sun as he forced a smile. "Is there any particular reason my ship is gone?"

Gibbs startled to attention and looked around. But Jack was most assuredly right—the *Pearl* was far out at sea.

All the while, Scarlett and Giselle had continued to bicker and their increasingly loud chatter was beginning to grate on Jack.

"Girls! Will you PLEASE! Shut it!" he shouted, whipping around to face them, his hair beads and bangles jingling. The women froze as Jack continued. "Listen to me. Yes, I lied to you, no, I don't love you, of course it makes you look fat, I have never *been* to Brussels, it is pronounced 'e-gree-ge-us,' no, I haven't met Pizarro but I love his pies, and all of this pales to insignificance in light of the fact that my ship is gone! Savvy?"

SLAP! Jack's head snapped to the side as Giselle struck him across the face.

SLAP! His head snapped to the other side as Scarlett now struck him.

Then, both girls stormed off, leaving a rather put-out Jack Sparrow behind them. A moment later, Gibbs followed.

Meanwhile, *aboard* the *Black Pearl*, Barbossa stood at the helm, his face tilted up to the sun, a smile on his wrinkled face. The remaining members of what was once Jack's crew—Ragetti, Pintel, Cotton, and Marty—stood nearby, eyeing him suspiciously.

"Sir," began Pintel, "some of the men don't feel entirely settled about leaving Captain Jack behind. . . ."

"Again," Ragetti added.

"Is that so," Barbossa asked, his eyes gleaming dangerously.

Pintel stammered and sputtered before

continuing. "It would make us feel a whole lot better regardin' our fortunes, if we could see that item you told us about."

Ragetti once again piped up. "To help put an ease to our burden of guilt, so to speak."

Barbossa looked around at the ragtag crew. While they may not have been the most clever of men, they were all he had. Barbossa began to slowly unroll the weathered charts Sao Feng had given Will. "Cast your eyes over this, then, mateys," Barbossa said. "There's more than one way to live for-ever." As he finished speaking, he opened up the charts completely and gasped. There was a hole!

Jack Sparrow had outwitted him . . . again!

On another part of the Caribbean, in a much smaller boat, Jack Sparrow looked at the very chart Barbossa was missing. As the map rotated and twirled, it revealed a drawing of a fountain, below which was inscribed *Ponce de Leon*.

Smiling, Jack pulled out his Compass and flipped it open, ready for wherever his next adventure would take him.

Epilogue

Ten Years Later

High atop cliffs, looking out over the sea, a young boy raced through the high grass, his voice carrying on the wind as he sang a pirate chantey.

Behind him, a woman appeared, her brown hair glowing red in the light of the setting sun. As Elizabeth watched her son sing and play, she smiled. Then, she raced after him and together the two continued the song.

Suddenly, the boy stopped and looked out. The sun was about to dip below the line of the horizon and, for a moment, Elizabeth and her son stood absolutely still, afraid to breathe as they watched the glowing orb drop lower and lower and then . . .

A flash of green!

Out on the sea, a familiar and long-absent shape appeared. Will had returned.

Just as he had promised.